"JUTHT CALL ME BUDDY. EVERYBODY DOETH."

"I go by Bubba."

"I know."

The elevator doors opened on the fourteenth floor, and we stepped into an empty corridor. A window down the way looked out onto the tops of familiar buildings, and the new perspective made me feel dizzy. I followed Buddy down the hall and waited while he wormed a card key out of his pocket and used it in the lock.

I motioned for Buddy to go first, and was slow to pull the door closed behind me. Not that I didn't believe there was a show-business type who wanted protection somewhere in the suite. Just trying to be careful.

A television silently flashed its picture in one corner of the room. The furniture was low and heavily cushioned, and pastel prints hung on the pale mauve walls. A door stood open to reveal a king-sized bed in the next room. Behind the bar, stirring a Bloody Mary, stood Elvis Presley.

"Steve Brewer gives a fast-paced and ⸻ it might be if America's No. 1 celebrit⸻ve. *LONELY STREET* and its Bubba Ma⸻ful new entry in the Private Eye field."

⸻an

Look for Steve Brewer's ne⸻
featuring Bubba Mabry,

Baby Face

Coming soon from Pocket

LONELY

STREET

INTRODUCING BUBBA MABRY, P.I.

Steve Brewer

POCKET BOOKS

New York   London   Toronto   Sydney   Tokyo   Singapore

This book is a work of fiction. Names, characters, places and incidents are products of the author's imagination or are used fictitiously. Any resemblance to actual events or locales or persons, living or dead, is entirely coincidental.

An *Original* Publication of POCKET BOOKS

POCKET BOOKS, a division of Simon & Schuster Inc.
1230 Avenue of the Americas, New York, NY 10020

ISBN: 0-671-74734-7

First Pocket Books printing June 1994

10 9 8 7 6 5 4 3 2 1

POCKET and colophon are registered trademarks
of Simon & Schuster Inc.

Cover art by Stephen Peringer

Printed in the U.S.A.

To my wife and inspiration, Kelly

LONELY
STREET

1

Limelight has always settled heavily on my family's shoulders. It began with my grandfather, or at least that's as far back as I've cared to trace this particular family trait. He was the only person who died in the Martian invasion in "War of the Worlds." That would qualify him for martyrdom in most invasions, but since "War of the Worlds" was a radio play, it only made him look stupid.

My grandfather, Pincus Cutwaller, a stiff-backed Mississippian who developed a device that squeezed more oil from cottonseed, made his first and only trip to New York City in 1938, to pick up an award from the American Society of Inventors. It was a proud moment as he waved farewell from the back platform of the train as it departed Nazareth, Mississippi. It was the last time his family would see him. His only daughter—my mother—was then nine years old.

The American Society of Inventors being the prestigious group it is, my grandfather was put up in a suite on the fourteenth floor of the Waldorf-Astoria. The room had such an excellent view that he spent most of his time standing at the window, watching the city bustle.

I believe he was standing there when an excited radio announcer first broke in with news that Martian space-ships were laying waste to the New Jersey countryside. The news must've startled him terribly. They found him splattered on the sidewalk before Orson Welles revealed, heh-heh-heh, that this was only a fiction created by Mercury Radio Theater.

My mother always clung to the belief that he fell. He must've been leaning out the window, she always said, trying to get a glimpse of those spaceships, and he just slipped.

Of course, this position made my mother all the more amusing to the newspaper reporters who stopped by our house once she became something of a media oddity herself. You might remember her as "the Jesus Lady from Nazareth, Mississippi."

Her real name is Eloise Cutwaller Mabry. She was a good mother in most ways. Just a little eccentric, maybe a little overly religious. Sorrowful portraits of bleeding Jesus hung on most of the walls of our house. Later they were replaced by framed front pages from supermarket tabloids featuring my mother's visitations from the Lord.

The visits began in late 1967 and ended less than a year later, but they defined my mother's life, for her and for the world.

The first visit came late one night when my mother was sitting alone in the kitchen, fretting. She often sat up late, muttering to herself about people who'd ruined her family's reputation by insisting her father had been fueled by fright when he went flying from that hotel window.

She looked up from her coffee to see a man, a personage, illuminated in the hall that framed the back door. The man had flowing brown hair and a thick beard

2

and his face was tan and gaunt. A light seemed to burn in the back of his eyes.

He said, "Why are you still awake? Did you know I was coming?"

My mother said later she was unable to answer, unable to break the lock with his eyes.

She said a lot of things, unfortunately saying many of them to the local newspaper editor, who soon had reporters from TV stations and tabloids breathing down our necks. People drove slowly past our house, and you could just feel them pointing and telling their children about the strange woman who believes Jesus visits her. Hysterical women and old black people would stop by with messages they wanted her to give to Jesus. Soon the house overflowed with gifts and flowers and cards and sacks of mail. When the newspapers reported that Jesus seemed most interested in the items of food and paid hardly any attention to the letters, supermarkets' worth of groceries began showing up at our door.

Of course, that's when the grumbling started in town. But the fact is my mother wouldn't let us touch one crumb of that food. She saved it all for Jesus' visits. And who would be brave enough to swipe something from the cache of Our Lord? What if it interfered with someone getting a blessing, a cure for a disease or something? Anyway, it will suffice to say Jesus got his pick of the goodies and we ate the same old grits and salt pork.

Reporters staked out our house, but Jesus wouldn't come if anyone other than my mother was awake. He somehow knew if someone was watching, which added to the mystique.

Finally, of course, Jesus slipped. He wandered out of the house, his belly full and my mother wondering at the fractured parable he'd struggled to tell her, and walked right into the hands of the sheriff.

Jesus turned out to be a hippie who'd built himself a wigwam in the woods, or at least that was the police

3

version. The fervent man never answered to any name other than Jesus Christ, and he seemed confused about which Nazareth he'd landed in. They tried to charge him with fraud, but the judge freed him on his own recognizance (if you can't trust Jesus, who can you trust?) and Jesus disappeared.

My mother couldn't just let it lie. She couldn't accept that she'd been had by an LSD-addled wildman. She insisted it really had been Jesus, and the police had made a terrible mistake in handcuffing Our Lord. That kept the headline writers cranking for a while. And it was enough to run off my old man, a long-haul truck driver who just stopped coming home from the road. After that, we scraped to get by. Still, my mother didn't learn her lesson. She kept talking to reporters about Jesus. Once a year or so, one would stop by our old frame house in the woods and interview Mama about "the visitations." I still see the occasional anniversary story in the Albuquerque papers.

Out here, of course, folks don't know about my connection to "the Jesus Lady" and I don't spread it around. I try to live my life as quietly as possible. I'd always hoped the Cutwaller curse of infamy would skip a generation.

The gullibility my mother and her father shared is not the kind of trait you want to pass on. Maybe that's why I've never had any kids, never even been married. If it's in the family line, maybe it will stop with me.

Maybe that's also why I decided to become a private eye. If I'm gullible, I tell myself, if I've got that terrible Cutwaller gene, then I won't make it long in this business. So I keep testing it, keep double-checking everything, trying to make sure I'm not being fooled. And if I am fooled, I keep quiet about it.

Truth is, I never really expected to make it as a private eye. And that's nearly been the case. The work has been so sparse over the past few years that I've spent more time reading paperbacks about private eyes than I have doing actual investigating. But jobs trickle in and I manage to keep afloat.

The trick to any kind of fringe business like this is low overhead. I may have the lowest overhead of anyone you've ever met. I work out of my Central Avenue kitchenette, which costs less than three hundred a month. I drive a twenty-year-old Chevy Nova (Spanish for "no go") that costs me nothing but gas and insurance. The only business expenses are the five-hundred-dollar license fee the state wants every year and my ad in the Yellow Pages: "Wilton 'Bubba' Mabry, Confidential Investigations, E. Central Ave."

Central Avenue has been sort of a hobby of mine since I first came to Albuquerque fourteen years ago. I was just a kid then, fresh from the Mississippi piney woods, beginning a four-year hitch in the U.S. Air Force. I was assigned to Kirtland Air Force Base as a military police-man. Since it was peacetime, I spent most of my time standing beside a brick kiosk, waving cars through a gate.

Albuquerque had seemed something of an arid para-dise to me then. There were mountains, for one thing, and no humidity and few mosquitoes. The people car-ried a frontier mentality, rugged individualism, that was different from the repressed plantation-owner/slave/white-trash class structure I'd grown up with in Missis-sippi.

I tried to go back. Not to stay, but to visit my mother and the few cousins who haven't joined the diaspora that's put finger-licking Southern rednecks in even the most cosmopolitan American cities. Even if I hadn't wanted to join that migration and escape the humiliation of being descended from Cutwallers, I would've had no choice. Life in the desert had spoiled me. When I went back to the South, it was as if I had malaria. The humidity made me sweat and swoon, made my clothes stick to my body as if I'd showered fully dressed. Once I completed my tour, it was clear Albuquerque, or some-place like it, would have to be my home. It's too cold up north for my thin skin, and the South now seemed as damp and hot and impenetrable as the Amazon basin.

So I stepped off the safe confines of the base and into the city I would claim as my own—unemployed, underskilled and largely unmotivated.

Being a military policeman prepares you for a career as a cop on the outside, and that's about all. Growing up around potbellied cops right out of a Burt Reynolds movie had persuaded me law enforcement wasn't for me. Besides, I was sick of uniforms.

So I went where all unemployed pilgrims go when they arrive in Albuquerque—Central Avenue.

Central is better known as old Route 66, famed in song as the place to get your kicks. These days it's more of a place to get kicked. Or beat up or stabbed. At least that's the case on East Central, where I live.

In the late 1960s, years before I'd even heard of Albuquerque, the interstate highways bypassed the old boulevard, forcing the city to lift up its skirts and settle down farther north. All the subsequent growth, which was considerable, occurred around the crossroads of I-25 and I-40, or somewhere along their shoulders.

Old neon-lit motels along Central had defined Albu-querque for years as a pit stop on the way to California. They suddenly found themselves empty, their business lost to Ramadas and Holiday Inns and Motel Sixes along the freeways. Ownership changed, rates were slashed and the motels began a slow slide toward deterioration.

Nowadays the motels are owned by families from India and Pakistan and freaking Zanzibar for whom owning their own businesses, no matter how ratty and run-down, is the American Dream. They're unbothered by a clientele of bikers and hookers and dope dealers and drunks.

Bharat "Bongo" Patel, the Hindu who owns the Desert

Breeze Motor Inn, where I live, is as placid and friendly a man as you'd ever want to meet. Smiling at whores as they check in for an hour at a time, gladly selling individual cigarettes to winos for a dime apiece. But hint that Bongo might not get his rent on time, or that a check might bounce, and his face goes even darker and his brows knit and you get the itchy feeling that curved knives could be in your future.

Not that I hold it against him. Business is business. And if it weren't for ambitious immigrants like Bongo, we fringe dwellers would be without a roof over our heads. A Sun Belt city like Albuquerque regularly rips out the old to make room for the new and more expensive. Bongo's people are holding the line.

So Central Avenue and the hot pink archways of the Desert Breeze have become my home. I like to think living among the criminal element and recent immigrants teaches a person tolerance. It also teaches suspicion, the perfect counterbalance to gullibility.

Which brings me back to this Elvis business. Like I said, I've lived here a long time now and any number of street people along Central might've sent his pal Buddy to look me up. No one's admitted it, and I don't blame them, considering how it all turned out.

2

I was finishing a shave with a disposable razor that was past its prime, carefully trying to reach the whiskers that hide in the cleft of my chin, when Buddy knocked on my door.

I went to the door wearing only my jeans, dabs of lather and specks of blood mingling on my face. My hands were empty, but my old snub-nosed Smith & Wesson sat on a low table behind the door. In this neighborhood, it's good to keep it handy.

If I'd known what was to come, I might've just picked it up and shot Buddy on the spot. Put him out of my misery.

"Mithter Mabry?" Something about the way his thick lips worked told me this was a lifelong impediment.

"Yes?"

"I'd like to talk to you. I think I might have thum bithneth for you."

"What?"

"A job?"

8

"Oh sure, come in."

I backed away from the door, angling to the right to keep close to my revolver. "Have a seat."

Buddy barely fit into the thrift-shop armchair in the corner. He settled daintily between the chair's arms, let them hug close the rolls of fat that started just below his armpits and ended somewhere near his knees. His brown hair was slicked back from a shiny pink forehead and he wore a loose jacket and tight pants of after-dinner-mint green, what they used to call a leisure suit.

He practically dripped gold jewelry—rings and a watch and a bracelet that said "Buddy" and a couple of chains that nearly hid among the folds of flesh under his chin. The jewelry told me two things. One, Buddy, if that was his name, had money to spend on whatever "bithneth" he was bringing my way. Two, he either didn't know the neighborhood or was foolhardy. That much gold, passed through a pawn shop, could keep a junkie supplied for weeks.

I found a towel to wipe the lather from my chin.

"Now," I said, "what can I do for you?"

"Well, I hope I've come to the right perthon." He intertwined his fat fingers in his lap. "Have you done much in the way of thecurity work?"

"Some." To say anything more might reveal too much. If this guy had money to spend on security, I was willing to take it, even if my usual jobs were more along the lines of snapping Polaroids of cheating husbands. Security was easy. Long as I didn't have to wear a uniform.

"Could you be available for thuch work now?"

"You mean today?"

"I mean thith minute."

"Depends on what it is."

"Of courth. But it'th pothible you could be available?"

"Well, I'm sort of between assignments. I might be able to squeeze something in, if it's the right kind of work."

9

In fact, it had been nearly three weeks since I'd had any kind of assignment and I had just been worrying about where I was going to find the money to keep Bongo happy. The first of May was just around the corner.

"I work for a thelebrity who happenth to be in Albuquerque at the moment," Buddy said. "Thomebody hath been harathing him and we think adding exthra thecurity for a few dayth would be a good idea."

"Who's the celebrity?"

"Then you want the job?"

"I don't know. Depends on who it is and who's bothering him."

Buddy looked perturbed.

"I'd rather not thay. Thith thelebrity liketh to keep a, uh, low profile."

"Uh-huh. So you want me to drop everything and go with you, and I'll find out who and what and where once I'm committed to doing it."

"If that theemth unreathonable, perhapth I thould look elthewhere."

"Hold on. Don't get your bowels in an uproar. It's not that I don't want the job. It's just an unusual way to go about it, don't you think?"

Buddy had no answer. He seemed to be thinking over whether he'd disclosed too much.

"How much does this job pay?" I asked. After all, "how much" was more important to me than "who." Always is.

"How doeth thirty dollarth an hour thound?"

My stomach flopped.

"It sounds like you've got yourself a security man. Let me get a shirt."

I fetched my favorite shirt off the peg behind the bathroom door. It's a heavy flannel, navy blue with lines of color shot through it to make an open plaid. I usually wear it with the tails hanging out so I can tuck the Smith

& Wesson into my jeans at the small of my back. It was getting too warm for the shirt, but I couldn't bear yet to put it away for the summer. I smiled at the thought of the new shirts I could buy with Buddy's money.

Buddy was silent in the other room. I checked my teeth in the mirror as I buttoned the shirt. I was beginning to get a bit of a tan, and Bongo hadn't even opened the motel pool yet. The way my hairline is receding, there's more of me to tan all the time. Fortunately, I'd gotten Mabel, a mulatto hooker who lives in my building, to give me a free haircut only a couple of days before and I looked almost respectable. I stuck a tatter of toilet paper on a nick, then went into the other room, rolling up my sleeves.

"Thath what you're wearing?"

"What's wrong with it?"

"Nothing. Ith jutht that you might, you know, not blend in tho well."

"How am I supposed to know? You won't tell me where we're going."

Buddy cleared his throat, setting his jowls to trembling.

"Thorry. You'll be fine." He waved his fat hands in a sort of blessing.

"I always dress this way. People don't look at you if you're wearing casual clothes. They don't pay any attention. That's the way I prefer it."

I don't know now why I felt insulted. For thirty dollars an hour, I'd wear clown shoes and a propeller beanie. But I felt compelled to hand out some fashion advice of my own.

"If I were *you,* I wouldn't come into this part of town wearing so much jewelry. You could get mugged."

Buddy grunted to his feet.

"I don't worry about that." He smiled without showing any teeth. "I can take care of mythelf."

"Is that a fact?" I let him see me stick the pistol in my belt and secure the clip-on holster. I arranged my shirt-tails and said, "Let's go."

It was one of those spring days in Albuquerque when the sun glares in a cloudless sky and the yucca is in bloom and the wind blows about sixty miles an hour. Buddy hustled across the parking lot, the wind snatching at his clothes. He moved surprisingly fast for someone built like a slug.

I hopped into the passenger side of a tan Cadillac Seville with tinted windows after Buddy popped the power door locks. Leather upholstery caressed my body. I closed the heavy door gently, shutting out the howl of the wind so completely that the sand and litter seemed to whip across the parking lot under their own power.

I had plenty of leg room even though the seat was adjusted for Buddy, who was several inches shorter than my six feet. He couldn't get closer than arm's length to the steering wheel because his huge, polyester-slick gut pressed against it. He looked like he could steer with that thing.

"Oh, thereth one thing. I almotht forgot."

He tried to lean across toward me, but was pinned by the steering wheel. He huffed and said, "Can you get thomething out of the glove compartment for me?"

"Sure."

I turned the latch and the door fell open. Inside, a revolver similar to mine lay on top of a Manila envelope and the usual assortment of registration papers.

"That envelope ith for you."

Central Avenue, gold jewelry, Cadillac, now practically handing me his gun. Never seen anybody so careless. No wonder these people needed protection.

I opened the envelope and pulled out a single sheet of white paper. It was some sort of boilerplate with a place for me to sign and date at the bottom.

"Ith a thtandard form. You thwear you won't write a

book about the thelebrity or talk to the media about him." Buddy shrugged. "Thath thow bithneth."

I glanced over the form. It seemed to be exactly as he said. Writing a book about an encounter with a celebrity hadn't even occurred to me. But once he mentioned it, I suddenly wasn't sure I wanted to sign that form. I always try to keep all my options open. Buddy handed me a gold ballpoint. I leaned over so I could use the dash like a desk and clumsily signed the form with my left hand. Buddy didn't seem to notice.

I might as well get this out of the way: I know wrong-handing my signature doesn't get me off the hook legally. A deal is a deal and I'm breaking it by writing this now. But the way I see it, they didn't live up to their end of the bargain either. Besides, I don't expect anyone to ever take me to court. They've got more to lose than I do.

I put the form back in the envelope and handed it to Buddy, who tucked it inside his jacket. The engine leaped to life enviably, and we headed downtown.

Albuquerque doesn't really have a skyline. Its office towers are scattered—some downtown, some uptown, even a few sprinkled along Central, right in the motel district. The biggest cluster of so-called skyscrapers are downtown in the Rio Grande valley, the lowest point in a mile-high city. The Sandia Mountains, two miles high, dominate the view so completely that buildings seem puny in comparison. I guess the city's architects figured that out a long time ago, and never got too ambitious. At least not until recently. Two buildings went up downtown a couple of years ago. One's the Hyatt Regency and the other bigger one is an office tower. They have matching, stylish peaked roofs that stand out above their flat-topped competitors. The taller one, tallest in Albuquerque, is something like twenty-two stories. Mississippi has taller buildings than that.

It was to these pink marble pride palaces that Buddy took me. The workday had started and most people were indoors, safe from the wind that roared through the empty streets. Somebody had lost a newspaper and its pages flew through the canyons between the buildings like a flock of pigeons. One page wrapped around the Cadillac's antenna and flapped like an ambassador's flag as Buddy steered us into the parking garage under Albuquerque Plaza.

After he squeezed the car into a slot, Buddy removed the newspaper page and carefully wadded it up into a ball with his pudgy hands.

"I hate newthpaperth. I hate everything about them."

He looked at his hands, which were black with ink, grunted and tossed the paper ball into the bed of a nearby pickup truck.

We silently rode up an elevator and popped up like gophers in the lobby of the Hyatt. As Buddy had predicted, I felt a little underdressed amid the plush carpet and chandeliers, but we crossed the lobby quickly and got into another elevator.

It was just the two of us, so I said, "Want to tell me now who it is we're going to see?"

"Maybe it would be betht if we left nameth out of thith. You'll probably recognithe him, but don't call him by name. It maketh him nervouth. He'th regithtered here as Mithter Aaron. You jutht call him *thir.*"

That rankled a bit, but I told myself I'd call him Your Royal Highness as long as I got my money.

"Jutht call me Buddy. Everybody doeth."

"I go by Bubba."

"I know."

The elevator doors opened on the fourteenth floor and we stepped into an empty corridor. A window down the way looked out onto the tops of familiar buildings and the new perspective made me feel dizzy. I followed Buddy down the hall and waited while he wormed a card key out of his pocket and slipped it in the lock.

I motioned for Buddy to go first, and was slow to pull

the door closed behind me. Not that I didn't believe there was a show business type who wanted protection somewhere in the suite. Just trying to be careful.

A television silently flashed in one corner of the room. The furniture was low and heavily cushioned, and pastel prints hung on the pale mauve walls. A door stood open to reveal a king-size bed in the next room. Behind the bar, stirring a Bloody Mary, stood Elvis Presley.

3

I knew it was him (or an extremely good impersonator) immediately. You don't grow up in Mississippi, the King's birthplace, without being deluged by his image. Not that I'd been a big fan. I'm not much on music myself. I usually use my transistor radio for sports.

By the time I reached high school and began paying attention to popular music, Elvis was in his polyester-jumpsuit phase and somehow didn't appeal. We didn't have much to be proud of in Mississippi, but Elvis was one item, and he didn't have to embarrass us by dressing like Liberace. Least that's how we felt at Nazareth High.

My interest, like everybody else's, peaked briefly when his sudden death was reported in 1977. But the story quickly got ugly, with allegations of drug abuse and suspicions about the coroner's report and rumors the King had been enthroned when he strained his way to a heart attack.

I knew there was a whole cult of people who refused to believe such an ignominious end. I'd seen a poll on TV that said something like seven percent of all Americans believe Elvis is alive. I'd seen the bumper stickers: E. P. PHONE HOME. But I'd always assumed it was just wishful thinking. I'd never even considered he might be alive. And I certainly never expected the secret to be revealed to me, the grandson of Pincus Cutwaller.

The living Elvis had let his hair go gray, part of his disguise, I suppose. But it was still the same *shape*. The sideburns, the forelock, the sleek sides. The gray looked funny streaking back from his sideburns, out of place in a haircut better suited to a juvenile delinquent than to a man who'd be sixty years old any minute now. His face had held up better, still smooth and high-cheeked, with that Cupid's bow mouth. He was a little thick around the middle, but trimmer than when he'd supposedly died.

Best of all, to an old Nazareth High alumnus, he was wearing regular clothes—designer jeans and a loose-fitting golf shirt. He had the same taste in jewelry Buddy had, but I guess that was to be expected. What do you do with a fortune when you're a fugitive? Wear it on your body. Would Elvis Presley still have a fortune? Had he stashed enough away before he "died"? I got a little internal flutter at the prospect.

The surprise must have registered on my face. Elvis looked amused, like he'd seen it all before. He cocked his upper lip into that famous sly smile and winked and said, "Want a drink?"

"Sure. I think I need one." He smiled more broadly and dropped some ice cubes in a glass.

I looked over at Buddy, but he was no help. He just grinned the way Elvis did, enjoying the moment. I guess it happened so rarely, them letting somebody in on it, that they got a kick out of it. My knees felt rubbery and I slid onto a bar stool.

"Buddy tells me you're from Mississippi." Elvis mixed the drinks as he spoke. I nodded and tried to close my mouth. "That's the main reason we picked you."

Elvis' voice sounded as smooth and nasal as it had in all those bad movies he'd cranked out in the Fifties and Sixties. Just enough baritone to make you feel rock 'n' roll could break out any minute.

"I wanted someone with, um, Southern sensibilities."

"I've got the right pedigree, but I don't know how sensible that makes me." I didn't want to come off too flip, but my mouth was sort of operating on its own. I was overwhelmed by the sight of a dead man pouring tomato juice.

"I like the way Southern people operate. We're always polite, you know, well-mannered, but, um, *effective.*"

He put an edge on the last word as it scissored through his smile. Something about it made me uneasy. Looking back, I should've realized that for someone as big as the King to have lived underground virtually undetected for fifteen years would require a certain amount of ruthlessness. But at the time I was too stunned that he was up and walking around. I suppose he knew that. If he knew anything about the Cutwallers (and I suspect that sometimes), he would've counted on it.

I said something automatic about always getting the job done as Elvis handed me my drink and motioned for me to follow him to the sofas in the main part of the suite. The window overlooked Civic Plaza with its fountains and acres of gray concrete and the excavation for some new building, where ant-size men dodged yellow earth-moving machinery. They were always building something downtown, but nobody but office workers and tourists ever came down here.

Elvis saw me looking and said, "Albuquerque. How long you been living here, Bubba?"

"Fourteen years or so. Long enough to know my way around."

"I was thinking before you got here about what a funny word that is, Albuquerque."

"It's Spanish."

"Uh-huh. And Mississippi is Indian. You only live in places with funny names?"

"Never thought of it that way, but, yeah, I guess so."

Elvis grinned again. "Course, about every place in this country's got a funny name, if you look at it that way."

"Guess you've seen 'em all, huh?" My mind was beginning to click. He'd have to keep moving. Even the most isolated spot gets visited by mailmen, delivery people, plumbers. Somebody would eventually recognize him. He could never stay long in one place.

"A few." Elvis seemed to read my thoughts. He didn't want me thinking too hard about the logistics. He set his drink on the coffee table and got down to business.

"I suppose Buddy told you I'm being harassed."

"He mentioned it."

"As you might guess, my privacy is of utmost importance. If anyone learns that I'm who you think I am"— he grinned—"the press would come swooping down on me and my life, the way I've chosen to live it, would be over."

I glanced at Buddy, who looked angry at the prospect.

"When I sent Buddy to find you, I had planned for you to just stick close to us and keep an eye out for anyone who might be getting close."

"A bodyguard," I offered.

"More like a bird dog, if you'll excuse the expression. Buddy guards my body just fine. I was going to have you tail us to make sure nobody else was. Flush 'em out."

"I see. But something changed."

"Right. After Buddy left, I got a telephone call." He gestured to the phone on the side table, as if offering proof it had happened this way. "And I found out where this guy is staying. So now I'm thinking we'll have you watch him instead."

"Surveillance instead of security." I was all business now.

"Right. Same fee okay?"

"Yes, *sir.*" There, I'd said it and it hadn't hurt a bit.

"I'm in the middle of some, uh, delicate negotiations here in Albuquerque." He smiled at the way the words rolled off his tongue. "It won't take long, but it's important nobody messes in my business while I'm here."

"You want him scared away?"

"You mean rough him up? No, that's not necessary. I want you to be a polite Southerner at all times." He leaned back on the sofa, stretched his arms along its back. He smiled over at Buddy, then back at me.

"You probably won't even get a chance to speak to the man. I don't want him to know you're watching. Just keep an eye on him and report his movements to us. We'll be able to tell if he's getting too close or going to the media."

"And if he does?"

Elvis' eyes glittered. "Then we'll decide what to do next."

I must've gulped or something because he quickly added, "I don't think it'll come to that. The guy seems harmless. He's just a fan who's clinging to the past. This kind of thing comes up from time to time in show business."

Or the no-show business, I thought.

What I said was this: "How did you handle it the other times?"

Elvis gave me that hard look. This was a man accustomed to getting his way, no questions asked. Before he even answered, I knew I'd made a mistake and I'd better keep my mouth shut if I wanted my money.

"This *particular* situation hasn't come up before." He spoke with finality, and I bobbed my head like the village idiot. "But in similar cases, let's just say we've been polite but effective. Just like I want you to be."

He leaned over and jotted on a pad of Hyatt stationery. He ripped off the page and handed it across to me.

"That's the fan's name and the motel where he's

staying. The phone number is ours here at the hotel. I'm, uh, usually in."

He smiled at me and I found myself smiling back, and it was all so damned conspiratorial that I believed it despite myself. Look at the guy. He's freaking *Elvis*. No question. And I'm helping him out, helping him keep his secret from America. Such a secret. I'm one of the very few who know he's alive. I got a thrill of power, of inclusion, of being part of the team. I stood up and pumped his hand and told him I'd get right on it.

On my way out the door, I said over my shoulder, "It's, uh, been nice meeting you."

He grinned and swung his hips to one side, playfully cocked a finger at me. Like it was a pistol. Like I was his audience.

"Thank you. Thank you ver' much."

I was in a daze as I followed Buddy back to the Cadillac. I stared out the window as we glided through the sunny streets. The wind appeared to have let up some, though tumbleweeds still bounded across Central near the boarded-up brick buildings of old Albuquerque High.

"You okay?" Buddy asked. I glanced over, but he kept his eyes on the road.

"Yeah, just a little stunned, I guess."

Buddy chuckled. "Motht people react that way."

"Are there many? Who meet him, I mean?"

"Damned few." Buddy's face went serious as soon as he'd spoken and he slammed his fat lips shut. His job rested on revealing nothing, and his expression told me mine did, too.

We were almost to the Desert Breeze before he spoke again.

"Thee thith car?" he said suddenly, startling me a little. "Mithter Aaron gave me thith car. Jutht gave it to me. He liked the way I handled a, um, problem for him one time. Tho he gave me thith car."

"It's a great car."

"It thure ith. Every time I drive it, I love that guy even more."

Buddy blushed at this confession, then barged ahead.

"Mithter Aaron liketh to give people thingth. He callth them bonutheth."

I barely followed that, but I nodded eagerly.

"If you do your job well, maybe he'll give you a bonuth."

He pulled the car into the cracked asphalt lot in front of the Desert Breeze and stopped. I ran my hand along the leather-bound dash of the Cadillac, smelled the car's sweet aroma. The thought of owning such a car suddenly filled me with lust and envy and greed. I swallowed hard and nodded, showing I understood the many possibilities the world could offer.

"When people don't do their jobth, Mithter Aaron geth very upthet. I've theen him be very, um, *aggrethive* when he doeth'nt get hith way. Do you follow me?"

I nodded. This part I had sensed.

"What about you, Buddy? Are you an aggressive person?"

"Not me, boy. I'm your *friend.*"

I must've grinned.

"Theriouthly."

4

Don't get the idea I'm some closet boozer, but when I got to my room, I went immediately to the kitchen shelf where I hide the bourbon. I only keep it on hand for medicinal purposes, for use in times of great shock or illness or depression, or the occasional rainy day. I find it handy to keep a double shot glass upside down on top of the bottle. Saves searching in times of emergency. I poured it half full and downed it and poured another before I took a deep breath. Then I set down the bottle and sipped the second one.

I went to the front window and peered through the slit between the curtains. The wind-swept lot contained only the usual rust-spattered heaps. The dark-windowed Cadillac had vanished.

I had to ask myself whether it had all really happened. Here I was in my room with a drink in my hand. Maybe I'd had a hallucination or a blackout or something. I groped in my shirt pocket for the slip of paper with the address and Elvis' phone number. The smooth paper felt like magic between my fingers.

It was then, I think, that the Cutwaller connection first occurred to me. Now I knew exactly how my mother must've felt when she looked up from the kitchen table and saw Jesus in the doorway. What an awesome thing! To be singled out for a face-to-face revelation from a great, even if dead, celebrity! (One dead much longer than the other, granted, and hers was the Son of God, so that counts for a lot. But mine was a thrill, too.)

Of course, I was lucky enough to know how her transcendent experience had turned out. I had no intention of becoming a nationwide laughingstock.

The thought that this Elvis thing could all be an elaborate hoax sobered me right up. I went into the bathroom and washed my face with cold water and combed my thinning hair. I've always thought of my hair as being a shade the peroxide companies would call "sheepshit brown." In retaliation for such ingratitude, my hair was packing up and moving on, starting at my forehead and working its way irretrievably toward my back. Looking into a mirror always got my mind off whatever problem I was facing, and got me thinking about my hair.

Here's what I decided while I was standing in the bathroom: Even if this guy's not Elvis, he's got me on the tab for thirty bucks an hour. For that much money, I'll play along as long as I can. I'll do my job like he was any other customer, and I'll take my money, and if I end up the butt of some stupid joke, that'll be just fine. If I like the joke, I'll laugh and shrug and take my money and go my merry way. If I don't like the joke, I'll laugh and shrug and take my money and maybe kick somebody's ass, but it'll be the same amount in the bank account.

Thinking about it this way made me feel tough and alert and suspicious. Polite but effective. I'll do the job and I'll watch my own back and all the while I'll keep my eyes open for any slip-ups that would show the guy wasn't really Elvis Presley.

And, what the hell, if he is Elvis, maybe I'll end up with a Cadillac. I was keeping my mind open. That's all I'm saying.

I gave my teeth a quick brushing to get rid of the liquor, then braved the wind to reach my old Chevy. Bolstered by booze and machismo and the keen edge of self-doubt, I was on the job.

My first stop, naturally, was the address Elvis had written for me: the Double Six Motel, a former Travel Inn that caters to people who get off the freeway and wander two miles down Carlisle Avenue until they find a motel on Central. This was not a big market, so the owner also did a trade with hookers. Thanks to him and his competitors across the street, this two-block strip remained one of the city's few true red-light districts. A block to the west, past the Planned Parenthood building, and you're into a strip of the trendiest shops in the city, reborn on Route 66. To the east, motels and car lots and used furniture stores march away toward the mountains. But right here, it could be any hooker district in any city in America—women in tight clothes looking for rides, johns shopping from slow-moving cars. The hookers call it The Cruise.

I didn't know the guy who ran the place, but I'd heard he was from Pakistan or Afghanistan, some freaking place like that. I pictured him as being like Bongo, small and dark and smiling and sneaky. I'd lean on him a little, maybe slip him a few bucks, and he'd tell me everything I needed to know about Mr. Harold Tankersley.

That was the name on the slip of paper Elvis had given me. I'd memorized the information, then carefully hidden the paper in my Gideon Bible. It wasn't much, but it was in *his* handwriting.

I parked the Chevy and walked across the lot to the lobby of the Double Six, looking around for any vehicle that might be following me, for any hidden cameras or microphones. Like most Americans, I harbor the secret fear that I might be suckered by "Candid Camera" for all the world to see. This Elvis thing would be just like something they'd cook up. Make a jackass out of a private eye in Albuquerque, New Mexico. Look, viewers would say, here's someone silly and prideful enough to think the living Elvis would seek his help.

No sign of Allen Funt. I rang the buzzer by the locked glass lobby door. Most business was done through a drive-up window and the owners apparently wanted to encourage that practice, but I kept buzzing until a woman in a sari came scowling to the door. She was small and the color of tea leaves, like Bongo, and she had a dot in the center of her forehead. More Hindus, I thought. These people I know. No reincarnation jokes. Don't offer a hamburger. Don't say, "Vishnu were here." The woman made a shooing motion with her hand, but I shook my head and smiled and made a threatening motion toward the buzzer with my finger. She unlocked the door and opened it a crack and said, "What you want?"

"I'd like to speak with the manager."

"You a cop?"

"Private investigator."

"Go away."

"Are you the manager?"

"No. Go away."

"Let's let the manager decide that."

"He not here."

"I could push this buzzer all afternoon. I don't have anything else to do."

She glared and huffed, but she let me in. The place was done in mismatched pseudo-wood paneling and the concrete floor was painted lime green. Sagging, gut-sprung furniture was arranged around a television in one corner. A metal stool topped by the Yellow Pages and a flat pillow stood by the drive-up window. A gaily patterned cloth curtained the door to the rooms beyond.

The Hindu woman shouted through the curtain in some other language. It sounded, I swear, like she said "Sucky-ducky."

A turbaned hulk ducked through the door. He was at least three inches taller than me and was built like a lumberjack. His skin was pale and his mustache was long, the tips waxed into near-circles. His hawkish eyes directed their glare at me. I was taken aback. I'd expected another half-pint Hindu, someone I could threaten. This was not that guy.

"Good afternoon," I said. I fished my P.I. license from my hip pocket and held it in front of his face. "I'm a private investigator," I said, in case he didn't get it. "I'd like to ask you some questions about one of your tenants, if that would be all right."

"Which tenant would that be?" He spoke with a British accent.

"Harold Tankersley."

"Why do you need information about Mr. Tankersley?"

"I have a client who says Mr. Tankersley is harassing him."

"How's that?"

"I can't say, really."

The turbaned one harrumphed and crossed his arms over his chest like he was guarding a harem. Maybe he was.

"I'd pay ten bucks for the information."

"Ten dollars is an insulting amount for a bribe."

"Sorry. It's all I have on me."

The woman had climbed precariously back onto the stool and settled onto her Yellow Pages. She was still barely tall enough to make a presence in the drive-up window, and the manager towered over her as they whispered in some clackety language. I heard him mention Tankersley's name, in English, so I knew we were getting somewhere. I got the sense the woman and the owner hated each other. Their conversation was brisk.

The owner turned back to me and said, "I know nothing of this man, but the woman says he checked in two days ago. He is only in his room at night. He has brought no one else there, not even a prostitute."

"Do you know where he's from?"

"We do not keep such paperwork. Ownership of the room key is registration enough for us."

"You must change the locks a lot."

"That I do. I also trounce anyone I catch using one of my keys without paying."

"That should work."

"It does."

"Which room is Tankersley in?"

"Number six, but he's not there now."

"What kind of car does he drive?"

He spoke sharply to the woman, who replied in kind.

"She doesn't know anything about cars. It's a blue rental. Bailey's Rent-a-Car."

The woman obviously did a good job keeping an eye on the place. I wondered briefly if she would watch Tankersley for me, but she didn't look friendly and I was pretty sure I didn't want to get in the middle of whatever was going on between her and the owner.

I reached for my wallet, but the owner said, "Don't insult me again." I thanked him and eased back out into the wind.

I'd parked my car around the corner, out of sight of the lobby, and it looked like I was returning to it as I headed for Tankersley's room. He'd left a light on, but no one answered my knock. The woman in the lobby was batting a thousand so far.

The chrome "5" on the green door of the next room dangled upside down from a single nail. It clattered when I knocked.

There was a long silence, then the door was snatched open so suddenly I about jumped out of my socks.

"Yeah? Whaddayawant?"

Lots of speed freaks live in these old motels. You can always spot them. Skinny, pale guys with long, greasy hair, dressed like bikers. Very high-energy, very twitchy, very temperamental. This guy fit all those descriptions except for the clothes. He wore only a black Metallica T-shirt and red nylon briefs. His room was dark and smelled funky and I could hear somebody else moving around in there.

"I said whaddayawant?" Mad already, mean.

"I, uh, I'm a private investigator. I'd like to ask a few questions about one of your neighbors."

"Don't know 'em. I'm busy now. Bye."

The door slammed shut about an inch shy of my nose.

I was a little hesitant approaching the door to Number Seven. Polite but effective, I muttered to myself, and I knocked.

I remember wondering, Why does it take these people so long to answer their doors? They're single rooms. How far away can they be? Then the door swung slowly open. A blonde stood in the shadows, her arms crossed, sizing me up. She wore very little clothing, and lace and satin made up what little there was. The first things I noticed, naturally, were her breasts, which were full and oval. They pushed against the transparent black fabric that half-covered them. A black lace g-string, black nylons and spike heels made up the rest of the ensemble.

"Come on in." Her voice was soft, husky, like everything she said should be whispered. "Shut the door."

The only light was what leaked in around the drapes. The room smelled of cheap perfume, something floral, and toothpaste. The bed was mussed, and there were enough beer cans and toiletries around to tell me she'd been staying here awhile.

She stepped up to me and threw her arms around my neck and pressed her mouth to mine. Her body fit nicely against me and her breasts felt warm through my shirt. I was surprised, of course, but I tried to relax and enjoy it. These cases of mistaken identity always sort themselves out soon enough.

She broke the liplock and let her head fall back, showing me her pale throat and her wet, open lips. It was too dim to get a really good look at her face, but it didn't matter. Her hands felt hot on the back of my neck. I found my hands around her lower back, fondling the flesh that bulged from under her g-string.

Her pelvis was tight against mine. She leaned back, watching my face for a reaction. She took one hand from the back of my neck so she could slide it up under my loose shirt. She dragged her fingernails down my chest and stomach. She stepped back just enough to give herself room to work, and was unbuttoning my jeans when I said, "My name's Bubba. I thought you might like to know."

"Mm-hmm." She contentedly lowered my zipper, unbothered by my feeble attempt to set things straight. She was peeling back the two halves of my pants, exposing my dingy briefs, when she caught herself and froze.

"I thought you said on the phone your name was Mike."

"I didn't call you on the phone."

My thumping heart stumbled a beat as she turned brusquely away. She picked up a pack of cigarettes from on top of the shabby dresser. She lit one, didn't offer to share, huffed out the smoke. She gave me a good going-over with her eyes, then said, "So you're not Mike?"

"No. I'm Bubba."

She opened a drawer and rummaged around.

"You got fifty dollars?" She didn't look at me.

"Not on me."

She turned from the drawer and brought a compact black automatic up level with my eyes. The hole in the barrel looked very large for such a small gun.

"Then what the fuck are you doing in my room?"

I'd been holding my jeans up since she stepped away, and when my hands shot into the air, my pants dropped to my ankles. I realized as soon as it happened that I'd put myself in a bad position. She hadn't even told me to put my hands up.

"I'm a private investigator. I just wanted to ask you some questions about the guy in Number Six."

"I don't know the fat slob."

"I, uh, I thought you must've mistaken me for somebody else when you, uh, kissed me. But I didn't really get a chance to stop anything. And I was kind of enjoying it . . ."

"But you're not Mike. And you don't have any money. Now get out."

She took a step toward me, holding the gun with both hands at arms' length. The right way. You might think a woman in skimpy black lingerie waving a gun around would be sexy, like the cover of a Mickey Spillane novel. But I'm here to tell you, it's not. There's a lot of weird stuff that might give me a boner, but not guns. My genitals were hiding somewhere near my liver.

"Can I pull my pants up first?"

"No."

I reached behind me ever so carefully and grasped the doorknob. I squeezed the door past my shackled feet. Then I shuffled backward out of the room, taking very small steps, nearly tripping over the threshold. She followed me, staying just out of reach, the gun pointed at

31

my face. As soon as I hit the sidewalk, she reached out with the barrel of the pistol and swatted the door closed.

The wind whipped my bare thighs. I squatted to gather up my jeans before I noticed cowboy boots approaching on the sidewalk. They came up to me and stopped. I looked up at a grinning redneck wearing a cap marked CAT. He had close-cropped black hair and jug ears and teeth big and white enough to have been stolen from a horse.

The redneck checked a slip of paper in his hand, looked at the number on the door, then looked down at me.

"Looks like I'm in the right place," he said. "Guess I arrived a little early." He paused, grinned wider. "Did you?"

I pulled up my jeans and busied myself with the zipper. If the guy noticed the pistol clipped to my pants, he didn't let on.

"You must be Mike."

"That's right."

"She's still waiting for you. We had a little misunderstanding."

It seemed impossible that his smile could get any bigger, but it did.

"Uh-*huh.* Well, if you haven't soiled the fair flower on the other side of that door, then I aim to."

"She has a gun."

"Then I expect I'd better be nice to her."

He yukked and hitched up his pants and reached out to knock. I stepped aside and pressed into Tankersley's doorway, wincing in anticipation of the shots I expected to splinter through the door of Number Seven.

The door opened only a crack this time.

"Mike?"

"That's me, honey."

She flung the door open and Mike stepped inside. I stood silently still as the door closed, waiting. Through the door, I heard Mike yell, "Whew-hooo-whee!" And I knew he'd been pleased by his fair flower. I felt a little pang of envy and regret. Why'd I have to go and open my mouth like that? I could've been Mike for a little longer. Of course, she probably would've shot me then, for sure. No way I could've come up with fifty dollars.

5

I'd had enough of the Double Six Motel. I returned to my car, climbed inside and spent a minute rearranging my hair where the wind had exposed the thin spots. That calmed my nerves, and I cranked up the old oil-burner and drove west on Central, hunting for Rodent.

I read something in a magazine recently about how the whole economy is turning to information. We're not *making* anything, we're just selling information back and forth. At first, the notion upset me, but then I realized some people have always profited from that kind of racket. Rodent's one of those people. He took advantage of a natural ability to pick up gossip on the street, just by hanging out and keeping his radar-dish ears open, and he'd made a good living selling to whomever was buying: cops, criminals, reporters, businessmen, people like me. It was understood by everyone that Rodent kept no secrets. He might rat on some street thug to the cops, then go to the crook and warn him the cops were after him and he'd better blow town. Two payoffs that way. A precarious business, but Rodent had survived a long time, and everybody'd sort of gotten used to him.

My personal feeling toward Rodent was that he'd be a waste of good spit. But there were times when nobody but Rodent could get information I needed, and I had come to more or less depend on him.

It wasn't sneakiness that earned Rodent his nickname, by the way. It was his looks. He had buck teeth and a pointed nose and huge ears. Even his shoulder-length hair was like a mouse's, sort of gray-brown and fuzzy.

I found Rodent outside a video arcade called Planet X. The sun was beginning to sink, and the wind was taking a breather. I stopped the Chevy in front of Rodent. He looked even scrawnier than when I'd seen him last. His black leather jacket barely clung to his narrow shoulders. He leaned over to peer in at me as I rolled down the window. Even in the parking lot, I could hear the growl and yawp of video machines.

"Hey, Rodent. How's it going?"

"All right. Just hanging, you know. Selling joints to schoolkids."

"What a guy."

"Hey, somebody's gotta do it. They *need* a little grass after a few hours in front of those video games. They get wound up with all that violence. You don't want them loose on the street like that, do you?"

Rodent could persuade you that providing bombs to terrorists would be a good way to make airline flights less crowded.

"Uh-huh. What's the word on the street?"

"Well, the word that doesn't cost you anything is that the cops are working a narcotics sweep up and down Central."

"So you pick now to sell pot?"

"Take advantage of the marketplace. Everybody else is too scared. I don't worry. I'm connected."

It was a fact, and he said it that way. No matter how

despicable the cops might find it, they needed Rodent on the street worse than they needed him in jail on some puny drug charge. He was safe. But *I* might not be. Whenever I chatted with Rodent I felt like someone might be watching. It made me edgy. Rodent didn't seem to notice.

"So what can I do for you today?" he said brightly.

"Ever hear of a guy named Harold Tankersley?"

"Nah. Must be from out of town."

"I think so. He's staying over at the Double Six."

"Then he's definitely from out of town."

"Think you could turn up anything on him?"

"I can give it a try. If it's worth enough to you."

"I've got a client who looks like a gravy train."

"Who?"

"Can't say."

"You know I could find out."

"He's from out of town, too."

"Doesn't matter."

"God, you're cocky today, aren't you?"

"Confidence is everything, man. How much?"

"Let's talk price after you see what you can turn up."

"Negotiable, huh?"

"Exactly."

"Dude's name is Harold Tankersley?"

I nodded, and Rodent patted the car door to show I was free to go.

"Hey, Rodent?"

He leaned over again. "Yeah?"

"You know much about Elvis Presley?"

"He's dead."

"Yeah, right. Never mind. See you later."

I eased the car out of the parking lot, and headed back the way I'd come on Central. I told myself I shouldn't even have mentioned Elvis to Rodent. It could've made him suspicious. Revealing any secret to Rodent would be like broadcasting it on the network news.

My next stop was Bailey's Rent-a-Car, which I knew was somewhere on Yale out by the airport. I wasn't in much of a hurry, so I drove west on Central all the way to the University of New Mexico before turning south. There were faster routes—Central had so many traffic lights—but I like to tool down Route 66, watching the sidewalks for hookers and coeds and street crazies and anything else that might be worth a gander.

The sky was alive with its daily show of color and fire. As the sun dropped behind the ancient volcanoes on the horizon, it dabbed orange on wispy clouds and made the sky go pale. Other than that, there wasn't much to see. It was that slow time of day when most people have made it home from work and are indoors, fixing supper.

I hit all the lights green as I drove south on Yale. Bailey's was on the corner with Gibson, which put it a little too far from the airport to be a success, despite its signs advertising extra-low rates. Guess Bailey, whoever he was, didn't want to pay for space in the newly remodeled airport, which was eight blocks uphill, through a gauntlet of coffee shops, motels, parking lots and competing rental car agencies.

I could see through the glass door that a pretty, twentyish brunette was working the counter. I broke out my smile and polished it off. Hadn't been using it much lately.

A doorbell said bong as I entered the agency. The counter girl's hair bobbed perkily as she looked up at the sound, an automatic smile on her face. She wore a blue dress that was some sort of standard-issue uniform, like a waitress's, and she wore a Bailey's tag above her left breast that said, "Hi! I'm Sandy!"

"Hello, may I help you?" She had a singsong lilt that comes from doing forced-to-be-cheery work.

I knew I needed to do something to knock her out of her automaton mode. Get her off-balance. I looked

STEVE BREWER

around the room conspiratorially, and she leaned forward to hear what I had to say.

"You could run away with me to Mexico."

She blushed and stepped back and made a sort of aw-shucks, get-out-of-here motion with her hand.

"I mean it. We'll go right up the street and catch a plane. We could sit on the beach somewhere, drinking margaritas and watching for whale tails."

"Whale tails?"

"Flukes, actually. When they dive, their tails come up out of the water."

"Oh." She seemed to ponder this, then said, "Well, thanks for the invitation, but I think Mr. Bailey would get mad if I ran away with a customer."

"The old tyrant."

She giggled.

"Well, I tell you," I said, sighing, "I'd much rather run away to Mexico with a pretty girl like you than do what I've been doing."

"And what would that be?"

"Oh, I'm a private investigator." I showed her my license. "I'm working on a case."

I watched sidelong for her reaction. They either get excited and think it's romantic and want to help, just like on TV, or they recoil in disgust and you might as well go talk to yourself. Depends on whether they've ever encountered a detective before and how much of a shit the guy had been.

The counter girl said, "Oh, so that's what this is all about," but her eyes shone with excitement. This was going to be easier than I thought.

"If you won't run away with me, you could at least make my life a little happier and help me with my case."

"How could I do that?"

"Well, the guy I'm investigating rented a car from here in the past couple of days, and I thought maybe you could give me some information about him."

"Mr. Bailey doesn't like us to do that."

"Boy, he is a hard case, isn't he?" She giggled again. Guess I had old Bailey pegged. "This could be your chance to get even with him, in a little way. And help out a poor old worn-out private eye at the same time."

I had her. She bantered it around a little more before she gave in, but I knew I had her. On the rental form, Tankersley listed an address in Vero Beach, Florida. The car, a Ford Taurus, was charged on a credit card that belonged to the Tropical Import Company. About the only other things the girl could tell me were that Tankersley took the full insurance package, which didn't help me much, and the license plate number, which did.

She'd been so helpful I was tempted to ask for her home phone number as well, but I looked at her eager young face and chickened out and thanked her and left.

It had been a long time since I'd even been tempted to pursue a woman. One of the down sides of living on the fringe is never having enough extra dough for dating. Lots of women don't see a good time unless it involves somebody spending money. I've met a few who were exceptions, women who became close to me, who were willing to overlook poverty and my other problems. But I've always managed to run them off eventually, through drinking or fighting or neglect or just moping around until they got fed up. I'm not a particularly jealous sort, but my potential for gullibility has left me with a squinty-eyed suspicion that some women find intolerable. And I suffer from a Cutwaller fatalism that fulfills its own prophecy by dooming relationships. These days, even flirting seemed too big a burden to bear. It comes with so much baggage.

When I got home, I checked in at the lobby. Bongo's son (a surly, chubby teen sometimes forced to stand duty while his parents were out) sat at the counter, reading a *Playboy* magazine. Framed portraits of Vishnu and Shiva decorated the wall behind him. They looked over his shoulder as he turned the magazine sideways for a better perspective.

I cleared my throat to get his attention, but he pretended not to hear. I slapped one hand down on the countertop, which made him jump, and he glared at me and closed the magazine.

"Anybody been asking for me?"

"No."

"You sure?"

"Yeah, I'm sure. Now leave me alone."

"Service with a smile, as always."

It sounded like he muttered "fuck off" as I was walking away, but I was in too good a mood to turn back and confront him. I made a mental note to suggest to Bongo that his kid could use the exercise of scrubbing out the pool.

I whistled as I walked across the parking lot to my room. Maybe it was my success with the Bailey's girl that made me so chipper. Whatever, I felt like I was clicking, like I wasn't missing a trick.

It wasn't quite seven, so I took a chance and called Lydia the Library Lady. The librarian who answered the phone said she thought Lydia was still around somewhere and went to fetch her. She was gone a long time.

I met Miss Lydia shortly after I became a private investigator. She already looked like a little old lady then, though she couldn't have been much more than fifty. She tried to teach me my way around the public library, but I was always hopelessly lost among the stacks. Finally, we developed this routine: I'd call the information line, where the public could get quick research for free, and ask for her. If I could make it interesting enough, enough of a challenge, she'd track it down for me. None of the usual tricks worked on Lydia. She considered herself beyond flirtation, and bribery attempts made her haughty. She lived only for the thrill of ferreting out obscure information. But to make certain I stayed on her good side, I also sent a fifth of bourbon down to the library every Christmas.

"Hello, Bubba." Lydia sounded a little breathless when she answered the phone. "I was downstairs."

"Still not using the elevator, huh?"

"Got to do something to keep me young. I don't want these bastards trying to push me into retirement."

"What are you doing there so late?"

"Oh, I got caught up in some research. Malaysian rubber plantations. Fascinating stuff."

"Uh-huh." I tried to think of a way to make my research project sound fascinating. Sometimes it's hard to tell what will push Lydia's buttons.

"What can I do for you today?"

"Well, I've got a new case and, uh, I'm stalking this guy, see, and I think he, uh, he might work for the CIA."

"Oh, really?" Piqued, but not fascinated.

"Yeah, I've got the name of the company he's supposed to work for—he has a credit card—and I was wondering if you could track it down."

"Oh, Bubba, that's too easy. Any of the girls here can chase down a business address. There's *Standard & Poors* and phone books and business directories of every stripe . . ."

"Yeah, but Lydia, none of those would tell me if this is a dummy corporation for the CIA or something like that."

"Well, what makes you think that might be the case?"

"It's in Florida."

"Hmmm. Could even be a drug connection then, couldn't it?"

"Sure." I tried not to sound too eager.

"All right," she said with a sigh. "I'll drop my rubber plantations and chase after your corporation. But it better not turn out to be just some run-of-the-mill business, or I'll be very disappointed."

Was even Elvis Presley worth risking my credibility

with Lydia? I decided to chance it, and gave her the name and address of the Tropical Import Company.

"I'll call you back," she said, still sounding less than intrigued.

"I'll be going out, but you can leave a message on my machine."

"I hate those damned machines."

"I know, Lydia, but I've got to go do some surveillance. I'll probably be gone all night."

She grudgingly agreed to call, and hung up.

I had another call to make before I could return to the Double Six Motel. Police Sergeant Larry Webster was well into his shift at the Northeast Substation at this hour, and I knew he might be able to do me some good.

Webster had been in the Air Force with me, also an M.P., but he'd taken the cop route when he got discharged. He was one reason I always felt I'd made the right decision, not becoming a cop myself. For years, he'd done nothing but bitch about his job, about how he wanted to get in an office somewhere and off the dangerous streets. He made sergeant a couple of years ago and moved indoors. Now he did nothing but bitch about working the night shift and the scum that tracked past his desk. It was always a treat to talk to him.

Despite all that, I kept on good terms with Webster, even went to barbecues with his family occasionally. I liked the guy, sure, but mostly I needed him. He had access to all the cop computers with their marvelous collection of information on anybody who'd ever so much as spat on a sidewalk. I could call on him sparingly, only on important cases. This was certainly one of those times.

"Northeast Substation." The woman who answered blurted the words. She sounded excited, and people talked loudly in the background.

"Sergeant Webster, please."

"He's busy." I heard what sounded like a crash, somebody yelling.

"I'll hold."

The chaos was replaced with the mellow Muzak of 101 Strings. I listened to three complete show tunes before Webster came on the line. Everybody I called sounded out of breath.

"Hi, it's Bubba. What's going on down there? You sound like you just lost a foot race."

"Aw, it's this goddamned paint sniffer we got in here. He went berserk and started tearing the place up. Pulled a fire extinguisher off the wall and kept everybody at bay with it for a while."

"He sprayed it everywhere?"

"Mostly he swung the fucking thing around his head. I thought he was gonna let go of it any second and kill one of these shithead patrolmen who were dancing around him. Then my ass would've been in a sling."

"So what happened?"

"Aw, somebody finally got hold of the fire extinguisher and the rest of them pounced on him. He fought like a panther. You know how it is with sniffers. They think they're fucking superhuman or something. I finally waded into the middle of it and sapped the sumbitch with my blackjack."

"Good job."

"Well, somebody had to do it. These fuckers would've wrestled with him all night." This last he said loudly for the benefit of whatever rookie patrolmen happened to be standing nearby. I could almost hear them hang their heads.

"Well, listen, I won't keep you, but I was wondering if you could run a check on somebody for me."

"Gee, I don't know, Bubba. It's crazy around here tonight. I don't know when I'd be able to get to it."

"Well, that's okay. Maybe in the morning, you know,

whenever. I'm just tailing the guy for a client, so there's no hurry."

Webster reluctantly agreed, and took down Tankersley's name and Florida address.

"All right, Bubba, but it may be tomorrow before I get back to you."

"I'm going to be out all night anyway. Whenever you can. Really."

It made my teeth hurt to be so understanding. I wanted something to carry back to Elvis, to show I was earning my thirty bucks an hour. But there's no sense pushing someone as irritable as Webster.

I also hoped the check on Tankersley might reveal something about Elvis and Buddy. I couldn't very well ask for new information on Elvis, and I didn't know Buddy's real name. Tankersley was my only lead in figuring out whether the whole thing was a hoax.

After checking my antiquated answering machine to make sure everything was set properly, I headed out the door. I bought some tacos (a luxury I allow myself only when I'm working; fast food is expensive), and hurried over to the Double Six. I angle-parked in a corner of the lot, facing out. From there, I could see Tankersley's room and the lobby and the street.

I'd finished my tacos by the time Tankersley's car pulled into the lot and stopped under the light at the lobby window. I couldn't see the license plate, but I knew it was the right car. It had that just-waxed, solid-color, chromeless rent-a-car look. I leaned over on one elbow so the top of my head wouldn't be so noticeable over the dash.

The car eased into a slot near Number Six and its lights died. A naked bulb hung above each room's door so I knew I'd get at least a glimpse of Tankersley before he'd get inside. He was mostly just a dark shape under the car's interior light as he gathered stuff off the seat beside him and clambered out of the car. I watched carefully, afraid to blink.

He stepped under the light bulb, keys in hand. He had six or seven newspapers tucked under his other arm and a white paper sack from McDonald's in his hand. A regular diet of fast food would explain his build, which was something like a milk jug. He was at least six-foot-two and weighed maybe three hundred pounds. Unlike Buddy, who looked like a balloon with a face drawn on it, this guy was big-boned and heavy-limbed and, well, *wide*. His head was a jumble of black hair, curly and long around his ears, thick around his chin and under his nose. He swiveled his head after he had the key in the lock, checking for anyone watching, and the movement reminded me of those films on Neanderthal men. Then he was gone through the door.

6

You see a lot of strange things in a motel parking lot. I watched one guy fumble with his keys while smuggling the biggest goddamned German shepherd I've ever seen into his room. The dog wore a leather muzzle and it looked worried. Two winos weaved through the parking lot and one unsteadily helped the other climb into a Dumpster. Then he wandered away, apparently forgetting about his friend, who never reappeared.

The traffic in and out of some of the rooms was incredible. I figured these girls must keep the switchboard lit up. If girls they were. I never really saw *them*, just one guy after another going in nervous and coming out smiling.

Other girls worked the neon-lit sidewalk on The Cruise, always two or three waiting for rides. The turnover was swift, giving me a steady parade of variety. It was like a fashion show for Frederick's of Hollywood, all satin hot pants and teddies and leotards and low-slung jeans. I looked with longing at the door of Number Seven, remembering the imprint of lace-bound flesh against my body. The traffic in and out of her room was slower than most, and that made me think about languorous lovemaking and that made my jeans uncomfortable.

The thing about a hooker is that she's had so much practice. With the least encouragement, she can outperform the average suburban housewife who's been working up to it for months.

Don't get me wrong, I've never paid for it. I mean, I know all guys say that, but in my case it's true. But that doesn't mean I haven't accepted the occasional charity tumble from the girls in the neighborhood. Or at least I used to. Since AIDS hit town, I've pretty much kept my peter in my pants. The escapade with Number Seven reminded me how long it had been.

Tankersley didn't come out again. His light went out a little after ten, and I began to consider my options. I needed to call my client, for one thing. Then I needed to figure out a way to watch his door and sleep at the same time.

An unlit pay phone stood in the corner where the parking lot met the sidewalk. I stretched the kinks out of my shoulders as I walked over to it. The air felt as cool and smooth as a whetstone, keeping me razor sharp. I picked a quarter out of the pocketful of change I always seem to carry, and dialed the hotel number I'd memorized.

"Hello." It sounded like him, but I'd dialed in the dark.

"Hello, is this, uh, Mr. Aaron?"

"Yeah, who's this?"

"Bubba Mabry."

"Bubba. I was just wondering about you. How's it going?"

"Pretty good. I have our boy under surveillance. Took me all day to run him down, but it appears he's now bedded down for the night."

"You're at the motel I told you about?"

"Uh-huh. I wasn't able to pick him up until he got back here at suppertime. The owner says he's been in the room two days."

"That means I picked up on him as soon as he hit town." Elvis sounded like he was thinking it over. "We were lucky."

"How's that?"

"We first ran across Tankersley in another state. I'd been watching for him to catch up to us."

"How did you pick up on him?"

There was a silence. While I waited, I admired the round asses of two hookers who leaned into the window of a Camaro. They gave me an idea.

"Let's just say," Elvis finally said, "I have contacts here in town and they, uh, alerted me to this matter."

"You don't want to tell me, that's okay by me. I'm just watching the guy."

"Exactly. Look, I like you, Bubba, but there's no sense in you getting any deeper into my life than absolutely necessary. That's the way I run things. Understand what I'm saying?"

"I understand." I got nervous every time he got upset. The first image that came to mind was of my thirty dollars an hour getting up and walking out the door. When one guy, a freaking temperamental celebrity, no less, is your meal ticket, then his happiness becomes paramount. Imagine how Buddy must feel.

He said nothing, so I said, "I can see why you'd be concerned by this Tankersley. He's a monster."

"Yeah. They call him Hank the Tank."

Where had he heard that, I wondered, but I didn't want to piss him off by asking. There was a lot he wasn't telling me. While my mind kept busy with that, my mouth said, "I gotta tell you, when you told me he was a fan named Harold, I pictured some little nerdy guy in a bow tie."

Elvis chuckled.

"You should've told me the boy has his own zip code." He laughed some more.

"Buddy told me you pack an equalizer," he said. "You got nothing to worry about."

"I have a policy. Never shoot anybody after sundown."

"But Bubba, that's the best time to do it." He chuckled some more. "Not that I'd ever want you to shoot anybody. I'd prefer that you run."

"You got it."

"All right, Hoss, I gotta go. Keep an eye on the Tank, especially during the day tomorrow. I want to know what he's up to."

"I'll call you tomorrow."

"Fine. Bye."

I hung up the phone and pushed my hands into the pockets of my jeans. I felt sort of chilled and trembly standing on Central with the cars whistling by. Just hanging out, talking to the King. I laughed and shook my head. Then I went to talk to the hookers.

The Camaro driver must've been choosy or something, because he'd driven away alone. The two hookers stood hipcocked, scanning the traffic with eagle eyes, watching the herd of cars for the slow and the weak. One was a short, plump Hispanic woman with hennaed hair piled high and lacquered into place. She wore pink eye shadow outlined in blue and a black spandex miniskirt. The other girl had raccoon eyes and Keith Richards's complexion. Her lank hair had been bleached too many times, and she shivered in the chill air. I don't trust junkies, so I spoke to the other girl.

"Hey, *chiquita*, how's the traffic tonight?" I stayed just outside the circle of light cast by the streetlight overhead. It was the girls' spotlight.

"Never too busy for a big *hombre* like you." She grinned at me, showing a gold tooth in the front. Pretty bold for a hooker. It's a wonder some drunk hadn't tried to steal that. Maybe that's what happened to the original tooth.

"Well, I can't afford a date with a beauty like you. But I do have a little proposition for you."

She looked dubious, but she took a couple of steps toward me, willing to hear me out.

"See that car over there? The blue one?" She glanced over, then nodded cautiously. "I just want to make sure the owner of that car stays in his room all night. I figured since this was your corner, you might keep an eye on that car for me."

She cut her eyes to the empty Taurus again.

"How much?"

"I'll give you ten bucks and my phone number. Then I can go home and get some sleep."

She smiled. "Wouldn't you rather forget about the car and take me home with you?"

"All I have is ten bucks." I pulled the bill out of my wallet and showed her.

The smile disappeared. She shrugged and said, "Sure. I'll do it."

I gave her the ten and one of my business cards. "Thanks. Don't forget to call if that car moves."

She grinned. "I'll need a quarter for the phone."

I found a quarter in my pocket and handed it over.

"Okay, big spender, if he moves, I'll call you."

It wasn't the best system, I know. This hooker might pocket my money and never give Tankersley's car a second look. Or she might ride off with a customer and never come back. But there was a good chance she'd be hitting this corner once an hour or so, and that was probably enough. Tankersley was asleep. And even hit-or-miss surveillance beat sitting in the parking lot all night.

Away from The Cruise, Central was quiet. Storefronts were dark and it was chilly enough to discourage pedestrians. The empty street called more attention to the neon that glowed red and green and blue along the way: motels and shoe repair shops and saloons and the forty-foot marquee of the Hiland Theatre.

I yawned my way into the parking lot at the Desert Breeze and went straight to my room. My answering machine's red light glowed. I rewound the tape and listened:

"I hate these damned machines, Bubba. They, uh, they get me all flustered because I never know how much time they're going to give me. Getting flustered just makes me talk more, which makes me more flustered and, well, hell, you can hear for yourself. This is Lydia. I, uh, wanted to tell you I'm getting intrigued with this import company you asked me about—"

Beep! The machine paused and I heard the whir of blank tape, then another message:

"Damn it, Bubba, this thing cut me off. I'm never going to call you again unless I'm absolutely certain that you're home. God, I hate these accursed things. Okay, quickly then, I can't find your corporation in any of the usual places, including the Vero Beach phone book. I'm going home now to get some sleep. Tomorrow, I'll come in early and get star—"

Beep!

There wasn't another message. I went to bed.

7

My alarm clock jangled me awake before sunup. I skipped a shower, but did wash my face and shave. Then I put on yesterday's jeans and a fresh shirt and my battered denim jacket with the bleach spatters on the shoulder. I took the last five-dollar bill from the drawer where I hide my cash, and made a mental note to ask Elvis for an advance. Then I was out the door, headed for the Double Six.

The sky was just beginning to gray behind the black hulk of the Sandia Mountains. I turned away from the dawn and followed my headlights down Central. Even the hookers had turned in at this hour.

It was Friday, and in Albuquerque that meant rush hour wouldn't come until later than usual. On Friday, everyone who can swing it comes to work late and leaves early. I read in the newspaper that the most dangerous time to be on the freeways is four o'clock on Friday afternoon. By that time, many people have waited in line at liquor stores' drive-thru windows, then consumed the better part of six-packs on their way home. Getting an early start on the weekend. The newspapers and the police have been leading a campaign to halt drunk driving, but traditions die hard.

I stopped by a convenience store to fill my travel mug with coffee. It was bitter and thin, but hotter than molten lead, and it helped me wake up.

The lobby window at the Double Six was empty, but still lighted, as I crept by in the Chevy. I swung the car in a loop at the rear of the parking lot and backed into a slot across from Tankersley's room. His car was right where he'd left it. I thought about checking to see if the engine was warm, but a light came on behind his drapes about then and I kept still.

Nothing happened for another hour, except for the usual magnificent sunrise. I suppose *he* was taking a nice hot shower. I finished my coffee and wanted more, but I sat waiting. Finally, Tank's door opened and he stepped out, his hairy hands empty. He wore a silver windbreaker so big it should've said GOODYEAR down the back. He squinted at the sky, then rumbled over to the rental car.

I followed him out Central past the fair grounds, then north on Louisiana Boulevard. He stopped at a Burger King drive-thru for a sack of breakfast. I watched with envy, afraid to follow him to the window. Might get stuck waiting for change.

Back on Louisiana, he drove only a few blocks before his blinker went on and the blue Taurus bumped into the parking lot of a newsstand. The tiny place was tucked between other buildings and I didn't even know it was there. Tankersley found his way around pretty well for somebody who'd only been in town a couple of days.

He came out with three dollars' worth of newspapers under one beefy arm, climbed back into his car and drove away, apparently without noticing me idling in front of a deserted bookstore down the block.

I gave him plenty of room as he continued north. We

passed over I-40 into the traffic around the city's two big malls, a part of town I generally avoid. It's called Uptown, and it's one of the other places in town you'll find buildings worth looking at. New ones going up all the time. Seven or eight stories apiece, each a little more outlandishly postmodern than the last.

"Where you going, Tank?" I asked out loud. He'd equipped himself for a picnic, by the looks of it. I hoped he wasn't looking for a nice park where he could read his newspapers.

About that time, he turned right, into the parking lot of one of the office towers. I drove on past, took the next available turn and went up a ramp, trying to get a glimpse of the blue Taurus. The ramp emptied onto another parking lot wedged behind the one where Tank had turned. The lots were staggered up an incline, and mine was about six feet higher than his, with a yellow steel fence and concrete curbs to keep you from driving off into space. I parked looking down on Tank's car and the entire parking lot and the entrance to the black-windowed building it served. It was perfect. Of course, if he decided to leave, I'd have to drive the wrong way down the one-way ramp to catch him. But the view was worth the risk.

Tankersley faced the building's entrance. He spread a newspaper over his steering wheel and wolfed a croissant sandwich that looked like an hors d'oeuvre in his hand. I counted three as they came out of the bag and disappeared into the hole in his beard. He also had coffee and two little cartons of milk, one white, one chocolate. My stomach rumbled.

I watched Hank the Tank for the next three hours. It only took about half that long to figure out he was doing the same thing I was: surveillance. He looked up from his newspapers every few minutes to glance at the entrance. Otherwise, he didn't twitch.

One of my shortcomings as a private investigator is a

lack of patience. I'm never very good at just sitting and waiting, and that's mostly what my job is. Waiting and watching. I don't mind the watching, usually. People can be interesting. But watching someone watch a building gets tedious in a hurry.

Tank, with his food and his newspapers, clearly was here for the long haul. I decided to take a chance and go for a walk.

I stayed away from the parking lot parapet, out of Tankersley's line of sight, as I walked to the office building. The guardrail parted at the end of the lot, and some steps took me down to a sidewalk alongside the building. I found a side entrance. It was a typical empty office lobby, without so much as a napping guard. The walls were covered with some kind of mahogany veneer, real nice, and the tile floors shone.

The only communication with the visitor was a building directory mounted between the elevators. Most of the tenants were lawyers or accountants, firms that listed themselves as strings of surnames. Any one of them could have some secret connection to Elvis. But one name stood out: Jerry Finkelman, Creative Entertainment.

Thow bithneth.

I rode the elevator to the fourth floor and stepped off it just long enough to see Jerry Finkelman was well insulated by secretaries and a receptionist. Then I rode down a floor and gratefully located a men's room. When I got back to my car, Tank was right where I'd left him.

Feeling bold now, I cranked up the Chevy and drove out the other side of the parking lot, looking for a pay phone. A convenience store gleamed in the sun a block down Menaul and I pulled in and plugged a quarter in the outdoor phone and listened to it ring.

Elvis answered the phone. It still rattled me. It was like being able to dial Heaven.

"Hello, uh, Mr. Aaron. This is Bubba."

"Yeah, Bubba. What can I do for you?" He was brusque, as if I'd interrupted something.

"I just wanted to tell you—" What? That I was on the job? That I still can't believe it's really you? "That our man seems to have settled in one place for the day. He's conducting surveillance on an office building at 2400 Louisiana. You know anything about that building?"

It took a minute for him to answer. I feared I had pissed him off again by prying, but he finally came around.

"Mmm. Yes. That's very interesting. I was planning on going to that address tomorrow for a business meeting."

"That must be what he's waiting for."

"All right, I'll change my plans. Thanks for the warning, Bubba. I'll handle it. You can go back to watching him now."

"Okay. Uh, listen, I've been running into a few expenses . . ." I let my voice trail off in the time-honored manner of the marketplace.

"Well, why don't you drop by the suite tonight after you get our boy bedded down? I have a little cash on hand we could use to cover your expenses."

I thought, I'll bet you do.

"That'd be great."

"Okay, see you then."

He sounded almost chipper as he got off the phone. It wasn't until I was standing in the checkout line with my coffee and sandwiches that it occurred to me: How did he know I'd let Tankersley out of my sight? He'd said, "You can go back to watching him now." I wondered about that until it was my turn to pay, then forgot about it as I hustled out to the Chevy.

When I got back to my surveillance post, Hank the Tank was gone.

"Okay," I said aloud. "Let's not panic."

I stepped out of the car and scanned the parking lot in

case Tankersley had decided to relocate. No sign of him. I got behind the wheel and raced out of the parking lot. I circled the traffic-clogged block. Nothing. I drove back to my original surveillance post and parked. My only hope was that he'd done like I had—taken a lunch break— and would be back soon.

I drummed nervously on the steering wheel while I waited. My hands were on the verge of being bruised by the time the Taurus wheeled back into the lot. Tank drove into the same parking slot he'd occupied before. He produced a hamburger from a paper sack and began to munch. I relaxed, and unwrapped my own cold sandwiches.

The whole episode made me think of those old Warner Brothers cartoons where the coyote and the sheepdog punch a time clock each day before and after their shifts pursuing/protecting the flock. Looking back on it, I wonder, which of us was the coyote?

The lunchtime shuffle turned out to be the only excitement of the day. I watched Tank watch the building until dark. I watched him eat a huge dinner in a Denny's. Then I followed him home and watched his window until the light went out. Only the thought of my late-night audience with Elvis kept me awake through the tedium.

There was no sign of the whore with the golden tooth. I thought about trying to get one of the others to watch Tank's car, but I was out of cash. Besides, Elvis had told me to come by, so he knew nobody'd be watching the Tank overnight. If it's okay with him, it's certainly all right by me. I'd had enough for one day.

I found a parking space on the street near the Hyatt, and walked the rest of the way. The wind had kicked up, and I held my denim jacket closed as I hurried down the sidewalk to the hotel entrance. Downtown is so barren at night it always makes me think of neutron bombs.

Even the Hyatt lobby was empty, except for two well-groomed desk clerks who eyed me. I thought, if you snoots had any idea where I'm going. It made me want to giggle. The elevator doors hissed closed and I punched the button for the fourteenth floor.

Something about my murky reflection in the steel elevator doors made me think of my mother. I guess it was the way my nose thickens at the tip, just like hers. Anyway, my mind flooded with thoughts of Jesus of Nazareth, Mississippi, and Orson Welles and Martians and the dreaded Cutwaller gullibility gene. That, as they say in the military, wiped the smile off my face.

Elvis was dead. This impostor probably was just a friend of Tankersley's, having him watched as a joke. They're playing hide-and-seek in a strange city. But what's the connection to Jerry Finkelman, if any, and why is Tankersley watching his building? Even if this is Elvis (and something inside me truly wanted to believe it was), why would he risk exposing his secret to me just to keep an eye on a fan? And what were the business negotiations that drew Elvis to Albuquerque?

That question brought one more to mind, and it was the one that drowned out all the others, the one that made me throw out my chest and step off the elevator into possible mockery. The question was this: Is there a chance for me to make a lot of money here?

Buddy answered my crisp knock. The sight of him made me feel tall and slim and confident. I said, "Evenin'," just like Gary Cooper, and he nodded me inside.

I tried to take in every detail of the room, looking for anything that might tip me that Elvis wasn't who he pretended to be. A wig stand, maybe. A makeup mirror. Maybe a guitar, which everyone knows Elvis never really played, just used as a prop. But then I saw him sitting on the couch, one side of his mouth grinning, and I knew he was the real deal, despite fancy sunglasses that covered half his face. He took the glasses off when he saw it was me and set them on an end table. Handy in case someone else knocked on the door.

My mind felt calm and alert, but my heart raced and my palms sweated. I surreptitiously tried to take deep breaths as I eased onto a sofa across from the King.

Elvis asked how I was doing and I must've answered because he said, "Good, good. And how's our friend Tankersley?"

"All tucked in for the night."

"Good. Listen, I appreciate that phone call today. You saved me some trouble."

"No problem," I said, but I was thinking, what trouble? Why was it so important that he and Tankersley not cross paths?

Buddy remained standing, hovering around the little entryway. I wasn't going to be here long. If I was going to learn anything, it had to be quick. But what could I ask without Elvis getting mad at me for poking into his business?

"It must be a trip," I said finally.

"What?"

"Being dead. I mean, people thinking that."

Elvis allowed himself a grin.

"It's different, I'll tell you that. It'll change your perspective on things."

"Like what?"

"Oh, like what people think about you. Fifteen years ago, people were tired of Elvis Presley. He'd been in the public eye too long. He seemed burned-out, and he reminded people who'd grown up with him that they'd gotten old."

I noted the change in pronouns, but I wasn't sure it

meant anything. Didn't celebrities often talk about themselves in third person? Like royalty?

"But now people love Elvis again." He looked a little smug, like he always knew it would turn out this way. "There's all that publicity about his life and death, and they play his records on the radio. Give people a little time, a little distance, and they get nostalgic. You can't turn on the TV without seeing Marilyn Monroe and she's been dead thirty years!"

I leaned forward, put my elbows on my knees.

"But what do you get out of it? I mean, if nobody knows you're alive, then what good does popularity do you?"

"Well, I don't make any money off it, if that's what you mean. But I don't really need money. I took care of that a long time ago."

I felt my eyebrows rise expectantly, and tried to get myself under control.

"But there's other rewards," he continued without noticing me. "I've been to Graceland a couple of times, in disguise, and watched those people put flowers on the grave. I read the papers, the magazines, about people who're sure they've seen me in fast-food joints and at stoplights."

"What about that?" I interrupted. "You're not dead. Maybe they really saw you."

He shook his head.

"I'm hardly ever where they say I am. It's mostly just people who really would like to see me, imagining things. But that's a kind of loyalty, too, isn't it?"

Elvis leaned forward, so our faces were only inches apart. His breath smelled minty.

"Loyalty's very important to me, Bubba. And I've got loyal fans. Even after all these years. They don't need media hype or rhinestone costumes or gyrating pelvises. Just the music. And their memories."

He sighed, and his eyes looked a little misty. Then he straightened up and looked me in the eye.

"Loyalty is what I want from you, Bubba."

He snaked two fingers into his shirt pocket and dropped folded bills on the glass coffee table. I couldn't tell how many, but the one on top was a fifty, so that was promising.

"I was thinking about this money situation," Elvis said. "And I think I'd rather pay you a flat fee than have you account for every piddling expense. Thought we could call this here an advance toward your final payment. That all right with you?"

The fifty alone would cover my expenses for a week. "Sure, I guess so."

Elvis sat back and chuckled. "Well go ahead, boy. Pick it up and count it."

I did. Five hundred dollars.

"This'll do just great." My voice came out a grateful squeak.

"I want you to just keep watching ole Tankersley," Elvis said. "My business here will only take a few more days, then Buddy and I will be moving on."

Buddy nodded, setting off tremors in his fat. He looked unhappy, worried maybe. Elvis, on the other hand, seemed suddenly more relaxed. Giving me the five hundred made him feel good, I guess. Imagine how good giving me a Cadillac would feel!

I guess you could say I was blinded by the windfall. I found myself in the hall in front of the elevators with the money in my jeans and the rest of my questions unasked and unanswered. I told myself the five hundred answers in my pocket would have to do.

I remember whistling in the elevator.

When I got back to my room, I found this message on my machine: "Damn it, Bubba, I mean it, I'm never calling your place again. Uh, this is Lydia. I've exhausted all of our resources and everything they've got at the university and, as near as I can tell, Tropical Import Company doesn't exist. There, I made it before this infernal machine cut me off. Goodb—"

Beep!

8

The next morning, I came prepared with my own sackful of fast-food breakfast. The girl at the drive-up window looked peeved at having to break a fifty so early in the day, but all that change made my wallet feel comfortingly fat. The rest of the fifties I'd hidden in my room behind a double-locked door. I had plans to give most of it to Bongo in the evening, so I'd be paid up through May. The roof always comes first, then luxuries like new shirts and fast food and booze.

As before, Tankersley made two stops: one for drive-up food, the other at the newsstand. Then he settled into his surveillance outside 2400 Louisiana. Because it was Saturday, only a few cars decorated the lot and the one above it. I parked in the upper lot again, but farther away, sort of behind Tankersley. With so few cars around, an occupied one would be more noticeable.

The Tank had met my expectations so far, and I tried to relax, knowing I had a full day of sitting and waiting and watching ahead. Then Tankersley surprised me by getting out of his car. He went to the trunk, opened it and removed what I first took to be a bazooka. Then I realized it was a camera, fitted with a succession of lenses totaling more than two feet in length. Tankersley held the camera by his thigh, the way a robber conceals a shotgun, and slipped back into the car. He propped the lens on the steering wheel and focused on the office-building door. Apparently finding everything to his liking, he set the camera on the seat and went back to reading newspapers.

So that was his plan. Wait here until Elvis shows up, then capture his image on film. I tried to imagine how much a photo of the living Elvis would be worth, but I had no knowledge of the market and I left it at "a bundle."

Bad news, Tank. Elvis ain't coming. I grinned. Thanks to me, the King's secret would remain intact.

I watched him for another hour, getting increasingly bored. I thought for a while about trying to take a picture of Elvis myself, but I couldn't come up with a way to manage it. It was easier to be Elvis' private eye, to see myself as being on the side of right and good, protecting the great man's privacy, his right to be dead.

Once it was clear Tankersley was set for the day, I decided to make the investigation a little more *active*. I wasn't going to learn anything sitting here. I decided to toss Tank's room.

Looking back, I probably should've stayed in the parking lot, doing my job without question. Polite but effective. But it seemed a good idea at the time.

Not long after I became a private investigator, I learned how to pick locks. Nothing elaborate, but your basic lock-in-the-knob residential security system. A one-eyed locksmith named Manuel Ortega gave me a quick lesson in exchange for a favor I'm not revealing here. Locksmiths are sworn to secrecy about their trade, so I've always felt lucky I'd stumbled onto Manuel. I keep four steel picks in a leather pouch in my glove compartment.

I was a little rusty, so it took nearly fifteen minutes to crack the simple motel-room lock. No one was around, but I kept looking over my shoulder at the littered parking lot, half expecting a patrol car and the brusque treatment that would follow. Even private eyes aren't allowed to break-and-enter in broad daylight. My hands were sweaty and my shirt was damp and I was about to give up when the cylinder finally gave. I immediately slipped inside and shut the door behind me.

There wasn't much to see in the room. Some jumbo-size underwear in one drawer, the usual toiletries by the sink, a few shirts on hangers. He hadn't even left his suitcase in the room, if he had one. Nothing to reveal who he might be, or how he'd gotten on to Elvis. The maid had been by, because the bed was made and the trash can was empty. As I left, I made sure the door latched behind me.

Driving back out Central toward Louisiana, I saw Rodent slinking along the sidewalk. I pulled over in a loading zone and leaned across the car to roll down the window.

"Need a lift?"

"Nah, I'm meeting a guy."

"Got any news for me?"

"Not so far. Your boy Tankersley ain't made much of a splash since he hit town."

"He's the quiet sort."

"I'll keep hunting."

"Okay, thanks." I reached to roll up the window, but Rodent rested his hand on it.

"Hey, you know anything about some fat guy's been lurking around?" he asked me. "Lotta gold on him, drives a Cadillac?"

"Doesn't ring any bells," I lied. "What about him?"

"Nothing. I just keep seeing him around. See ya."

I wanted to ask a few questions about where Rodent had seen Buddy, but I didn't want to make him suspicious. I eased the Chevy back into traffic.

We seemed to be getting a break from a week of windy days, and the streets were busy with grateful tourists and yuppies running errands and middle-class housewives rummaging through the musty "antique" stores that have sprung up along East Central like mushrooms. The traffic got even thicker near the malls. First really nice day in a week, and people are swarming to get indoors and shop. Go figure.

I turned right onto Menaul and went half a block to the back entrance of the parking lot where I'd perch and watch Tank for the rest of the day.

Only he wasn't there. The empty parking slot where he'd spent the past couple of days seemed to mock me. At first I persuaded myself he'd taken an early lunch break. But as the minutes crept past, it became clear Tank was gone.

I waited more than an hour just to be sure, then cranked up the engine and pulled back out into the mall traffic jam. My anxiety added weight to my foot and I drove recklessly.

Normally, I wouldn't get so excited about losing a tail. Happens all the time. You just figure out where the guy is going next and pick him up later. But in this case the stakes seemed much higher. If I couldn't see Tankersley, maybe that meant *he* was seeing Elvis somewhere. Maybe he'd somehow learned Elvis had moved his business meeting and gone there. Since I didn't know where that might be, I was in a bind.

I finally swung off Central and the frustration of its traffic lights and got onto Copper, a parallel residential street that's a speedway for impatient people like me.

I could see before I turned into the back entrance of the Double Six Motel that Tankersley's car was not there.

I sat in the parking lot for an hour, giving him time to have lunch before coming home to his room, then drove back to 2400 Louisiana to check the parking lot. Nothing.

I had nowhere else to look. Because my feeble investigation had turned up so little on Tank, I had no other ideas about where he might touch down in Albuquerque.

What was I going to tell Elvis? He'd given me a simple enough job. Just watch Tankersley and phone in once in a while. He was paying me a lot of money to do it. But I had to go off playing Sherlock freaking Holmes, committing felonies in search of nonexistent clues, and what do I get? I lose the guy.

Tank would eventually return to the Double Six, I knew, so I headed back over there. But I stopped by my place on the way. The red light on my answering machine blinked at me. I rewound the tape.

"Bubba. Webster here. I ran that name through the computers and the only Harold Tankersley that matched your half-assed description isn't a crook. He's in the computer because he was issued a Florida state press badge. He works for the *Star News*, one of those supermarket weeklies. If it's the same guy. Big guy? Black hair?"

Beep!

My heart was pounding. I snatched up the telephone receiver to call Elvis right away. Warn him that Tankersley was roaming the city unwatched, could even be headed his way with his long-lensed camera. But I hesitated. Did I want to so quickly admit my failure? I remembered the hard glitter in Elvis' eyes when he'd talked about dealing with Tankersley if he became a problem. How would he deal with a screw-up like me? I set the receiver down.

Then it dawned on me. Elvis knew who Tank was. He had to. That's what this was all about. He and Buddy never thought Tankersley was some zealous fan. They knew exactly who he was and how much damage he could do.

The thought shook me a little, reminded me how little I really knew about what was going on. Elvis—if he's really Elvis at all—had kept me in the dark about nearly everything. My self-loathing was tempered a little by resentment. How did Elvis expect me to help if I didn't have all the facts?

Of course, now I knew some facts he didn't know I knew. That gave me an edge, but I couldn't think of any way to take advantage of it. The best way to make money on this deal still seemed to be the thirty dollars an hour from Elvis.

I remembered the way Elvis had talked the night before about his fans, about loyalty surmounting death. Suddenly I was more inclined to believe he really was Elvis and therefore deserving of my loyalty. If the guy was some kind of impostor, why would a tabloid reporter bother chasing him around?

Still, I decided to wait, thinking maybe I could pick up Tankersley again. Then I could call Elvis and say I'd found him. Give the good news first.

On my way back to the Double Six, I stopped by a convenience store for more cold sandwiches, a large bag of tortilla chips and a copy of the *Star News*.

I guess it goes without saying I'm not a fan of the tabloids. Usually I could give a shit about which celebrities were sleeping together in some distant universe called Hollywood. When the tabloids report phenomena —real or imagined—from other parts of the world, all I can think of is my mother and how she was exploited by those smartass reporters. Every UFO spotter and ghost hunter and religious fanatic in America could get written up in the supermarket tabs these days, only to be ridiculed by neighbors and shunned by mortified relatives.

Those people don't deserve such treatment. They

really believe they saw Jesus' face in the bubbly surface of a tortilla or that their children are demons or that big-eyed aliens captured them and probed their bodies. Who's to say what's real and what isn't? I've seen plenty of strange shit along Central that could easily make headlines in the *National Enquirer* or the *Weekly World News*. Once or twice, I've even thought about calling them, see if they pay good money for story tips. But I never have. Pride is an expensive commodity, but you have to draw the line somewhere.

The *Star News*, fortunately, seemed concerned entirely with movie stars and rock musicians. No common people to be exploited. I'd always figured celebrities sort of deserve whatever they get in the tabloids. They get paid plenty to put up with adulation. But sitting in the parking lot, paging through the *Star News*, I began to have second thoughts. No one gets paid enough to have his bowel problems written up in depth, complete with drawings of polyps and rectums. I think some aspects of a person's sex life should be private, too. I certainly wouldn't want all of mine exposed.

People don't get to have secrets anymore. And secrets are too valuable, too necessary, to give up.

I studied the photographs of celebrity couples emerging from restaurants, searching out the tension behind their automatic smiles. People ought to be able to go out to dinner without flashbulbs blasting in their faces.

Something like outrage welled up within me. I began to see Tankersley (damn his missing hide) as the enemy. These scandal sheets have gone too far, I decided. Nobody deserves this kind of personal scrutiny. No wonder Elvis decided to be dead. No wonder he doesn't want his secret revealed. Even life underground would be an improvement over photographers in your shrubbery.

I didn't think about it at the time, but I'm just as guilty when it comes to snooping. Hell, I've *been* the photographer in the shrubbery, plenty of times. I feel rotten about it sometimes, but a man's got to eat. Even now, though, I can't put myself in the same category with those tabloid reporters. At least when I pry into somebody's life, I usually only tell one other person—my client. Those guys broadcast their humiliations to the world.

Getting all steamed up didn't bring Tankersley's car swinging into the parking lot, but it helped me pass the time. Before I knew it, the afternoon was on its last gasps.

As it grew darker, I noticed Tank had left a light on in his room. There was something about the light that was different from the night before. It was brighter against the curtains, like its shade had been removed or tilted.

Curious, I got out of the car and slipped across the parking lot to Tank's window. I peeked through the crack between the curtains and could see the light bulb glowing. The lamp was on its side, its shade gone. I couldn't see anything else of the room, but that was enough. I fetched my lock picks out of the car. I remembered the feel of the lock and it was quick this time.

The room had been tossed, and whoever did it had either been in a hurry or didn't care about sloppiness. Clothes lay everywhere, drawers hung open and the bed had been stripped and slashed. A bottle of cologne was broken somewhere. The room reeked of Brut.

I reached to right the lamp, and hesitated when I thought about leaving fingerprints. Then I realized my fingerprints were all over the room from my earlier visit. I set the lamp upright. Its hot bulb left a charred place on the tabletop, so I knew it had been like this for a while. Hell, I knew that anyway. I'd been sitting outside all afternoon. Nobody had gone in or out. That meant the room had been searched around the time Tank had disappeared. I got a sinking feeling as I stepped over stuff to reach the bathroom door.

I flipped on the light and found the biggest, hairiest, whitest ass I've ever seen staring up at me. Hank the Tank was sprawled halfway into his bathtub, facedown on the porcelain with his pants around his knees. There was a lot of blood.

My first instinct at the sight of a corpse is to run. It's an uncontrollable response. I was at the front door, headed for the parking lot, before I got a grip on myself. I was panting, like all the oxygen in the room had been replaced by Brut. I tiptoed back to the bathroom for another look. My feet danced a little at the sight of Tankersley, but I kept them under control.

Tank had been taking a dump. The evidence still floated in the bowl. He'd been sitting on the throne and somebody had stepped into the doorway and blown him off his seat. The impact of the three bullets had thrown the big man sideways, over into the bathtub. I peered over into the tub and saw Tank's eyes were open wide. He looked startled. Clutched in his big fists was a blood-soaked copy of the *Star News*. I made out his byline at the top of the page. Reading his own copy on the crapper when the Man came for him.

Even the cologne couldn't cover the mingling stenches in the bathroom and I got out of there. I found the phone under a table in the other room, dialed and asked for Homicide.

9

I guess I was lucky Steve Romero was on duty. Aside from my irritable friend Webster, Romero may be the only cop in the whole APD I'd trust. Not that we're friends, really, even though we've known each other for nearly a decade. More like friendly acquaintances. We see each other only a couple of times a year. More often than not, there's a corpse nearby.

Romero's been a homicide detective for twenty years, and he's so accustomed to stiffs he seems to scarcely notice them when he enters a room. He's always friendly, shaking hands and talking quietly to witnesses. The whole time, his brain is sucking in clues like a vacuum cleaner.

He always knows just how to react. I've seen him come on like a saint comforting the mother of a dead hooker, and I've seen him grab a suspect's head in his huge brown hand and squeeze until the bastard passed out.

Romero is the last guy who'd ever be hoodwinked. He's maybe the least gullible person I know. But that didn't keep me from trying to lie to him on occasion. This looked like one of those times.

When I got him on the phone, I said, "Steve, this is Bubba Mabry." I sounded like my vocal cords needed tuning. "I've got a murder for you."

"Aw, Bubba, not now," he said good-naturedly. "I'm up to my ass in stiffs."

"Okay, I'll call back later. This guy's not going anywhere."

It was the right answer because Romero laughed. I felt some of the tension drift out the top of my head.

I gave him Tank's name and the address and hung up. I pulled to the door of Number Six and waited in my car.

As usual under such circumstances, I spent the time silently cursing myself for ever getting into this damned business. What was I going to do now? Somebody greased the Tank, and I'm known to have been asking questions about him, following him around. And my fingerprints are all over his room. It dawned on me then that I could've wiped the place down before calling Romero. I opened the car door, thinking maybe there was still time, and a squad car whipped into the parking lot, its red and blue lights flashing. I closed the door.

The Dodge bounced to a stop, and I watched two young patrolmen jump out, their hands on their holsters. Their heads snapped around as they hunted for somebody to arrest. They spotted me in the Chevy, but Romero's unmarked car arrived before they had a chance to rough me up. They looked disappointed, but immediately bowed to Romero's presence.

Near as I can tell, Romero wears short-sleeved Guayabera shirts year-round. They make him look even wider than he is. He's sort of square all over, like his head is a box set on top of a bigger box. He didn't bother with a jacket as he grunted out of the car and came over to shake my hand.

"Dead reporter, huh?"

"Using the term loosely," I said. I guessed the police computers had spit out everything they knew about Tankersley before Romero was halfway to the Double Six.

I started toward Number Six to show him, but Romero gently grasped my arm.

"Afraid I've got some bad news. I've been trying to call you."

Bad news? Before he could even tell me, I felt shocked. How much more bad news could I stand? And what could be so bad that he had to tell me before he'd even looked at Tank?

"What is it?"

"Rodent's dead. A bag lady found his body in a Dumpster behind the Running Indian Motor Lodge early this afternoon. I'd just got back from there when you called."

I staggered back against the car, let the fender catch me and prop me up.

"I'll be damned. What killed him?"

"Somebody shot him three times."

I felt woozy, like I might be sick. I teetered there against the car, unable to respond.

"At least that's the way it looks," Romero said. "They're doing an autopsy sometime tonight."

I couldn't see Rodent in my mind, dead or alive. The only image that came was of a drowned rat I'd once seen in a gutter outside the Desert Breeze after one of those hard summer rains that fill the streets. The creature had been the size of a house cat, even with its fur matted flat, and its lips were peeled back to expose sharp teeth. I'd been unable to sleep for a week after stumbling across that rat. Every squeak and stirring in the motel had caused me to start awake.

"You all right?"

I recovered enough to say, "Yeah. Why didn't you tell me on the phone?"

"You didn't give me a chance before you started telling me about another murder. Besides, I thought this was the kind of news you ought to break in person."

What he meant was he wanted to see my reaction when he told me. See if I gave anything away. That brought me back to my senses, reminded me I needed to stay on my toes. What I had in mind for Romero was a regular ballet.

"Wow, I'm really surprised," I managed. "I mean, I don't know why, but I'm surprised. I guess it was bound to happen sooner or later."

"What do you mean?"

"I mean Rodent, his line of work. He must've crossed the wrong person."

"Think so?"

"Sure. That must be it. You know how he was." The word *was* came a little too easily to my lips, somehow, and I wondered if Romero noticed.

"He been doing any work for you lately?"

"No. I ran into him this morning, but he didn't know anything about the guy in this room." I jerked my head toward Number Six.

"The guy's from out of town."

"Yeah. Otherwise, Rodent would've had something on him."

"That's right." Romero nodded and looked at his feet, as if in silent tribute to the recently departed snitch.

"Well," he said, looking up, "I guess we better go take a look at your stiff."

I didn't like the idea of Tank being *my* stiff, but I followed Romero to the room. A couple of residents had wandered outside to see what the commotion was about, but most of the rooms stayed dark. I saw one of the patrolmen down the way, arguing with the big turbaned owner. Romero muttered some instructions to the other patrolman about setting up a crime-scene perimeter, and then he and I went inside.

I watched Romero survey the damage from the sloppy search.

"You touch anything?" he asked without looking at me.

I'd been formulating an answer to that question and I took a deep breath and I tried it out.

"The phone, when I called you."

"Uh-huh."

"And, uh, I poked around a little, trying to figure out what somebody was looking for when they wrecked the place."

"Before or after you called me?"

"After. I called you first thing."

"Uh-huh." His eyes swept the room. "Where's the stiff?"

"In the john."

He carefully picked his way through the clothes and sheets on the floor and peered into the bathroom. I held my position near the door. I'd seen enough of the late Harold Tankersley.

Romero tiptoed into the bathroom for a better look, and I got a second to catch my breath. Rodent was dead. I couldn't get over it, yet I didn't necessarily believe it had anything to do with my case. Like I told Romero, he probably got caught in another double-cross, and the victim wasn't as forgiving as others had been. He'd told me he was going to meet a guy, and it occurred to me maybe I could track that guy down, but it would have to wait. I had troubles of my own, and fixing them would have to come first. Besides, I had a paying client, and that takes precedence over avenging a dead snitch.

I quickly went back over what I'd told Romero, and felt sure I hadn't revealed too much. Not yet, anyway. He was a long way from done with me.

He came back out of the bathroom, shaking his head.

"Man can't even take a dump undisturbed anymore."

Buying time, I asked him, "How do you think it happened?"

His brown eyes glinted. "You tell me."

"Well, I don't know *how* it happened, but I can tell you about *when* it happened. I was tailing the guy this morning. I lost him about ten o'clock. I hunted for him for a while, then ended up back here. His rental car wasn't around, so I waited. Finally, after the sun went down, I noticed the light was funny and I peeked through the curtains and saw that lamp had been tipped over."

I pointed to the charred place on the tabletop, and Romero nodded.

"I checked the door and it was unlocked, so I let myself in, set the lamp upright and found the body."

"When did you start waiting in the parking lot?"

"Around lunchtime."

"So, somebody had two hours to do this while you weren't around."

"Yeah, something like that."

"You didn't hear any shots?"

"Don't you think I would've mentioned that?"

He nodded. His head was cocked to one side while he studied me. My face felt hot, and I thought he could read on my face every little omission.

"I'll bet," he said after a moment, "that nobody else around here heard shots either."

"It's that kind of place." I thought he was talking about the seediness of the motel, but he was way ahead of me.

"Killer probably used a silencer."

"How do you figure?"

"He sure didn't toss the room while Tankersley was sitting on the crapper. And it looks like he thoroughly searched the place after he shot him. If he was worried about somebody hearing the shots, he would've been in more of a hurry."

I nodded admiringly. He continued.

"I imagine the killer didn't find whatever he was looking for in the room, so he took Tankersley's car someplace where he could search it, too."

I'd had more time to think about Tank's murder, but none of these deductions had occurred to me. I was so busy trying to protect my own ass, I hadn't even considered the sequence of events.

"Makes sense," I said, still nodding like a dashboard poodle.

"Any idea who did it?"

"None."

"Why were you watching him?"

"I've got a client who wanted him watched."

"And who's this client?"

"You know better than that, Steve. I've got to clear it with the client before I can reveal the name."

Romero's face darkened, but he said nothing. I felt suddenly twitchy.

"They're not going to like that answer downtown."

"Can't help it. My reputation's on the line."

"You've got that right. Think what a murder rap would do for business."

"You mean I'm a suspect?"

Romero pursed his lips, like he was trying to keep from calling me stupid.

"Your fingerprints are all over this room, right? You've been tailing the guy. Guy's from out of town. You're all we've got."

"If I'm the killer, then why did I call it in?"

"To cover your ass. To make it look like somebody else did it."

"Jesus, Steve, you know me better. I'd never shoot somebody in cold blood."

"Yeah, I know better. But my boss won't. You know how these things work, Bubba. You're the easy answer. And my boss doesn't think much of private detectives."

I fought off an urge to say "Yipes" or something to that effect. Romero shook his head.

"See, Bubba, it's like I've been telling you for years. You need to get away from The Cruise. You need to move uptown and get some real clients and make some real money. Quit living like a goddamned street person. I knew it was only a matter of time before you got caught in a situation like this."

"But I didn't do it," I squeaked.

"Doesn't matter. Unless we get some other fingerprints or luck on to somebody else, you're It."

I knew he was trying to scare me. He wanted me to hand him another suspect by blurting out my client's name. I said nothing.

"Let's get out of here," he said. "That cologne's making me gag."

The patrolmen had found somewhere a steel stanchion mounted on an old auto wheel, and had rolled it into place outside the motel door. Then they'd strung around it yellow plastic tape that read CRIME SCENE. DO NOT ENTER. We ducked under it on our way out.

Some of the hookers had put on their robes to come outside and sneak a peek and the patrolmen had their hands full keeping the growing crowd clumped in one area. The turbaned owner towered over the rest of them, glaring at me. A couple of other plainclothes cops had arrived, and Romero ordered them to begin questioning the residents.

I spent the next couple of hours sitting on the hood of my car, waiting for Romero to finish. The crime-lab boys came and went, and some guys from the coroner's office hauled Tank's huge body out, belted to a gurney. His stiff body wouldn't lie flat, and the sheet was barely big enough to cover him. They hefted him into the back of an ambulance and drove away. No siren. No need.

At one point, Romero came over to me and asked whether I was carrying my gun.

"Sorry," he said when I nodded, "but you're going to have to hand it over for tests."

"It hasn't been fired in months."

"Good. Let the tests prove that."

I handed over the Smith & Wesson, holster and all, and Romero put it in a plastic bag.

Later, he paused near me long enough to ask, "That door was open when you got here?"

"Yeah. It was pulled just to so it hadn't latched."

"Mmm."

"What?"

"Lock's scratched up like somebody jimmied it recently. Sloppy job of it, too."

I let the unintended insult pass, and tried to look bewildered. He went back to work.

Finally, Romero was done, and he jerked his head at me to show me I was riding with him.

Once we were cruising down Central toward Downtown, he said, "You sure you don't want to tell me about your client before we get to the station? They're going to try to play rough with you otherwise."

"No can do, Steve."

He nodded and said nothing else.

Romero was right about his boss, a red-faced old-timer named Morgan. He didn't like private eyes. Morgan had been called away from supper with the news of a murdered reporter, and he was not a happy man. I quickly became the target of that unhappiness.

Morgan and the others never touched me, though they came close, leaning over and yelling into my face. I answered all their questions as carefully as I could, all but the several hundred questions they asked about my client. Romero stayed in the background, looking thoughtful, keeping quiet. I kept wishing he'd jump in and defend me, but I didn't blame him when he didn't. Looking back, I'm probably lucky a hothead like Morgan was in charge, rather than someone as wily as Romero.

After two hours, I'd had enough. Morgan asked again about my client, and I surprised him by standing up from the wooden chair.

"Look, Captain Morgan, we've covered all this several times. I've told you everything I can at the moment. I'll have to talk to my client before I can say anything more. If you think you can make a case against me, then file the freaking charges. Otherwise, I think I'd like to go home."

Morgan reddened even more as I walked to the door. Romero was stone-faced, but I thought I detected a touch of humor in his eyes. A muscle-bound detective stepped into my path. Morgan motioned him away.

"Go ahead," Morgan sputtered behind me. "Walk on out. You're a free man. For now. We know where to find you."

I was outside the hulking police station in the cool night air before I remembered my car was at the Double Six Motel. Albuquerque's not exactly crawling with taxicabs, and I didn't feel like hiking a couple of miles, mostly uphill. I couldn't very well go back up to Homicide and ask Romero for a lift.

I was briefly tempted to cross Civic Plaza to the Hyatt and tell all to Elvis. But I knew Morgan would have somebody tailing me, just in case I was dumb enough to do something like that. I could practically feel the eyes on my back. It took me so long to make up my mind that I was almost afraid they'd arrest me for loitering. Finally, I set off up Roma toward the lights of the Doubletree Hotel. If they thought I was going to see my client, I figured, the Doubletree should give them a nice long guest list to check out.

The doorman frowned at me as I slipped into the lobby. I don't know why I always get that response from people. I hustled across to the phone booths and hid inside one of them, watching the lobby through the glass in the door. I first dialed Yellow Cab and ordered a taxi. Then I dialed the number I'd memorized for Elvis.

The phone rang four times, then there was a click and a woman came on the line. "Hyatt Regency Hotel."

"Uh, yeah, I was, uh, trying to reach Mr. Aaron in 1409."

"One moment."

A burly Hispanic in a windbreaker and jeans eased through the lobby door and made a big show of not looking directly at me as he walked toward the elevators. The girl came back on the line.

"Sir? I'm sorry, but Mr. Aaron has checked out."

10

I couldn't have been more stunned if she'd beaned me with a sledgehammer. I don't remember much about the trip home. I do recall asking for Mr. Aaron's forwarding address and learning that there wasn't one. I remember the cabbie seemed pissed off about something (but don't they always?), and I remember being relieved that my car was still intact at the scene of the crime. An unmarked Dodge followed me home.

Other than that, the next thing I knew I was in my room, sitting on my bed, staring at the wall. I felt very alone. It was a long drop from the exultation I'd felt when I was included as a member of Elvis' team. Now the team had abandoned me. Tank was dead. Rodent was dead. And I'm left holding a very large bag.

I kept telling myself the cops wouldn't have a case against me. My gun would pass the firing tests and the ballistics wouldn't match, and without a murder weapon they'd have to admit it wasn't me. But Romero's words kept flashing like neon in my head: I was the easy answer.

Now that Buddy and Elvis had disappeared, I was the *only* answer.

My phone machine was blinking at me and I hit the switch to make it stop. A dead man spoke to me.

"Hey, Bubba, I got a line for you." It was Rodent, sounding as cocky and street-smart as ever. "Did you know you're being followed?"

My heart jumped. I knew the cops were following me now, but this message had to be several hours old.

"Yeah, normally I'd make you pay in advance for this kind of information, but I figured you might need to know in a hurry. It's that fat guy I told you about, the one with the jewelry. I've spotted him tailing you a couple of times, so you might want to watch out."

"Beep!"

"Bubba, this is Steve Romero in Homicide. I need to speak to you ASAP."

Rodent had seen Buddy following me. How could I not have seen it? I was so busy chasing Tankersley around that I hadn't thought to watch my own rearview mirror. But surely I would've noticed that tan Cadillac drifting along behind me. I replayed Rodent's message, but he'd made no mention of a car. Maybe Buddy had swapped cars, gotten himself something more anonymous. That thought made me feel a little better.

If Rodent saw Buddy, maybe Buddy saw him. Maybe Buddy was responsible for both murders. It didn't seem like Rodent to be caught off-guard like that, but maybe I was giving him too much credit. After all, how smart could he be? He's dead.

I remember thinking, Rodent gave me a tip and I'll never have to pay him. He must be grinding his teeth in Hell.

I played the message again. The sound of wily Rodent's voice made my mind work. If Buddy was following me, then he knew when I went to toss Tankersley's room. He must've stuck with Tankersley instead of following me while I played detective. When Tankersley left the office building, Buddy must've followed him back to the Double Six and iced him in the bathroom. Just a matter of goofy timing that we hadn't all ended up in that room at the same time.

Then Buddy had searched the place and, as Romero had deduced, hadn't found what he was looking for. So he'd taken the Taurus. What could he have been looking for? What could a tabloid reporter have that Buddy would want?

The fact that he'd taken the car meant someone had helped him. He wouldn't leave his own car at the murder scene. The only someone who came to mind was Elvis Presley.

That brought me back to Earth. I was beginning to think I had a theory I could take to Romero. But I couldn't tell him about Elvis. He'd never believe it. I imagined Morgan's reaction. That would probably be enough to push him over the edge. An old-timer like him, he'd be getting out the rubber hose. And I no longer felt like I could count on Romero for kindness. He didn't believe I killed Tankersley, but I got the feeling he was so perturbed by my stupidity that he was willing to stand by and let them try to nail me for it. Probably for Rodent's murder, too.

Another consideration: The shitstorm of publicity that would erupt if the media got wind of this Elvis business. If I told the cops—even if they didn't believe it—somebody would tell the newspapers. It would be the end of the anonymous life I've built for myself. I couldn't put up with notoriety the way my mother had. I don't have as much conviction about Elvis as she had about the Lord. I'd have to duck out, go into hiding. I'd become like Elvis, living underground, always on the move. The only difference is that I wouldn't be staying in the Hyatt. I'd probably be sleeping in my car.

Only as I fully realized what a fix I was in did it occur

to me that somebody planned it that way. Tankersley's death had been orchestrated, and I'd stumbled right into it, unwittingly playing my role. For some reason, Buddy and Elvis needed to get rid of Tankersley, and I was the perfect fall guy. Unattached, with a less-than-terrific reputation, living on The Cruise, working on the cheap. Five hundred dollars was a bargain for somebody to take a murder rap.

And they'd found someone who was gullible enough to believe Elvis is alive and in need of help. I wondered briefly (as I have many times since) whether Elvis somehow knew about my connection to the Mississippi Cutwallers, about how easily we're buffaloed.

I was filled with self-hate and fear. How could I have been so stupid? How could I have let them set me up this way? What the hell am I going to do now?

I had plenty of time to think about it because I barely slept a wink. It actually wasn't that tough to sort out. I had two stiffs and two suspects. The suspects had vanished. Because I had been so cavalier about letting Elvis keep me in the dark, there was nothing else. No one else was involved in the case, unless you count the cops, and the hookers and assorted street people I'd talked to along the way. And I didn't have so much as a guess as to which direction Elvis and Buddy may have headed.

It occurred to me around midnight that the killer could come for me. Why not? If Elvis' devoted Buddy had offed the other two, he could see me as the final threat. I'd seen the living Elvis. I might risk the ridicule and tell the cops. Why not push in my door and pump three slugs into me like he had the Tank? And Romero had taken my gun. I got out of bed and fumbled around in the dark closet until I found an old taped-up baseball bat I keep there. I carried it back to the bed, and told myself I was now safe. But it's hard to sleep when you're afraid to get under the covers and there's an old bat in bed with you.

With so few clues to manipulate, there wasn't much for me to do but lie on top of the covers and worry. I walked through it again and again, trying to figure what I'd missed, trying to discover another angle, but it kept coming up the same way. Finally, near dawn, I resolved out of desperation to go see Jerry Finkelman at Creative Entertainment. He might have nothing to do with the case, but he was the only person who seemed at all likely to know anything about Elvis. If I turned up nothing from him, maybe I would question the rest of the people in the firms at 2400 Louisiana. How long could that take? A lifetime?

Meanwhile, I kept getting the icy feeling that Elvis was moving farther and farther away. In my mind's eye, the tan Seville grew smaller against the horizon, until it was a speck in the sunrise.

11

I was showered, shaved, dressed, coffeed and impatient by the time eight o'clock rolled around. That was the time I had set as being decently late enough on a Sunday to call Jerry Finkelman, whose number I'd found in the business pages with no address. I figured it was an answering service, but I lucked out and Finkelman himself answered the phone. He had a high-pitched, nasal voice that had Brooklyn stamped all over it. I still have the Southerner's distrust for anything Northern, but I concealed it as I persuaded him I had an urgent matter that had to be discussed in person. He sounded put out when I refused to wait until Monday, then agreed to meet me at his office.

Though I couldn't spot them, I figured cops were watching me, so I pulled some quick maneuvers through parking lots and alleys off Central, trying to shake them. When I was done, I still couldn't see anybody back there, so I drove to 2400 Louisiana.

It was nearly an hour past our ten o'clock appointment before a tomato-red Porsche pulled into Jerry Finkelman's reserved slot in the empty parking lot. It wasn't enough that he was a Yankee or that he was late, he had to drive that car. As a matter of principle, I hate guys in Porsches. Such displays of wealth are like peacocks showing their feathers or those big baboons with the inflatable multicolored asses that are supposed to arouse their mates. Whenever a Porsche roars past me on the freeway, I hold up my thumb and forefinger, very close together, to show the driver what I think about the extent of his manhood. They probably don't get it, but it makes me feel better.

Anyhow, there was Jerry Finkelman climbing out of his red Porsche, and it made it easy to come on tough with him. I blocked his path on the sidewalk leading into the building and introduced myself.

He looked me over. He was a pint-size, fortyish guy who stood with his head thrust forward, like he wanted someone to take a swipe at him. He had a big pointed nose and a receding chin. His wavy hair had been slicked back, so his whole head looked streamlined, like he'd been fired out of a gun nose first. He wore jeans, and a white shirt that might've been silk hung casually loose around his bony shoulders.

"You got any identification?" His tone made me want to give him a good shaking, but I showed him my P.I. license, then followed him inside to the elevator.

"I don't know what this is about, man, but it had better be good." Finkelman didn't look at me as he said it; he was watching the numbers above the elevator tick down to the ground floor. "I don't like my Sundays interrupted."

"Well, this might only take a few minutes," I said gruffly. "Then you can get back to your hot tub and your Perrier."

He arched an eyebrow at me, but didn't say anything. We rode the elevator to the fourth floor and the doors hissed open and I followed him through the darkened outer office with its empty desks and silent telephones. He flipped a switch as he went through a door and fluorescent lights buzzed and blinked on overhead, illuminating a smallish office with a largish desk. The room was decorated in George Jetson Modern, with a lamp that looked like Saturn and a desk with more buttons and gadgets than a cockpit. The walls were covered by rock posters of various vintages, most autographed and dedicated gushily to Finkelman. I slumped into a black leather hammock slung on a chrome frame, and Finkelman climbed up into the high-backed swivel chair behind the desk. He looked bigger back there, which I suppose was the desired effect.

"Now," he said regally, pointing his nose at a spot somewhere over my head, "what can I do for you?"

I'd thought about it during the night and had decided to stop trying to be clever. There was no time for that now.

"What can you tell me about Elvis Presley?"

Finkelman looked unsurprised by the question. I'd been hoping for some sort of reaction and got none.

"What is this, a history test? The man's been dead, what, seventeen years? What could I tell you that you couldn't look up in a book?"

I gestured to the posters and backstage passes that papered the walls. "I thought maybe you knew him."

"Nah. I was just starting in the business when he croaked. No way he would've had anything to do with a whippersnapper like me."

"What about more recently?"

Finkelman leaned across his desk and fidgeted some of his toys. When everything was where he wanted it, he looked up at me and said, "What are you trying to say? That the man is not dead?"

"I'm saying I sat this close to him two nights ago." I

was taking a chance, sure, but I could tell Finkelman wasn't going to give me much more time.

He sat back in his chair. His thin eyebrows arched up his forehead, his way of saying "Bullshit."

"It was either him or the best impostor I've ever seen." I still couldn't bring myself to say it was Elvis without backpedaling.

I told him quickly about Tankersley and how he'd watched this building, apparently waiting for Elvis. How he'd turned up dead, and how an informant was found killed the same way.

"I think this Elvis character or his sidekick maybe killed them both, but now they've disappeared and the cops are trying to pin it on me."

Finkelman studied me, his face still expressionless except for the skeptical eyebrows.

"That's all very interesting, but what does it have to do with me?"

I could see I was getting nowhere fast.

"Well, I thought you might've been the person Elvis was coming to see. You're the only company in the building in the entertainment field."

Finkelman webbed his hands in front of his chest and half-grinned at me.

"And you think Elvis would be contacting a promoter if he was living underground, not really dead?"

"Maybe. I don't know."

"I think I'd be the last person Elvis Presley would contact if he was still alive."

"Why's that?"

"Because I'd try to make a publicity splash with it, man. I'd try to get him to make a comeback. That doesn't sound like what he'd be looking for."

I mulled that one over. Finkelman swiveled back in his chair and put his feet up on the corner of the desk. He wore loafers without socks. He showed me his little pointy teeth.

"Yeah, I wish Elvis Presley would reveal himself to me," he said. "I could make a fortune out of it."

Because I wasn't making a fortune, the comment made me feel even lower than before.

"Well, I'm just trying to get off the hook on a murder rap."

He continued as if I hadn't spoken.

"I'd schedule a sixty-city tour with full promotion and advertising. We'd get him on the cover of all the news magazines with the story of how he faked his own death and managed to elude everyone for years. The networks would go nuts. We'd need to get him in the studio right away with some new songs so we could have a record hit the stores simultaneously with the concert tour."

He was ticking the items off on his fingers like they were so many things to pick up at the grocery.

"Sounds like you've got it all figured out."

"Sure. That's what I'd do with any celebrity that was supposed to be dead. Bring me Jim Morrison and we'd go the same route. Unfortunately, it never happens. Dead is dead."

He let his feet drop off the desk and leaned forward conspiratorially.

"But if you find this Elvis, and he somehow turns out to be the real thing, give me a call."

He grinned again, and I could tell he was pulling my leg.

"I think the cops will want first crack at him," I said, still trying to come off tough. "Not only are there two murders here to consider, but faking your own death is a crime."

Finkelman threw out his hands so they framed his pointed face.

"More publicity!"

He cackled and sat back and looked at his watch.

"Well, this has all been extremely entertaining, man,

but I really do need to run. It sounds to me like you've been the victim of a prank."

"Pranks don't end up with people dead."

The smile dropped off Finkelman's face. "Some do."

There was a heartbeat of a pause as I tried to read what he meant, then he said, "Good day, Mr. Mabry."

I opened my mouth to object, but he was right. We'd covered everything. I was wasting his time. I showed myself out.

12

I went back to the Desert Breeze, mostly because I couldn't think of anywhere else to go. Driving down Central, I spotted another of those obvious undercover cars a block behind me. I wondered if the cops had seen me at 2400 Louisiana, then realized it'd just send them on another wild goose chase if they had. Same goose I'd been chasing.

I was puffing, like hot anger had pushed out all my air. Anger at Buddy and Elvis for getting me into such a mess. Anger at myself for falling for it. Anger at Finkelman because he hadn't been any help.

I was back in my room, my shot glass in one hand and my anger medication in the other, when someone knocked. I set the bottle down, stalked across my room and snatched open the door.

She was a tiny thing, maybe five feet tall and a hundred pounds. Her shiny hair was cut off squarely just below her ears and was the same shade of brown as the rims of her square glasses. The thing I noticed was her eyes, which seemed to burn with the intensity of a righteous Iranian's.

"Wilton Mabry?" She bit the words off cleanly.

"Yeah?"

"I want to talk to you." Her lip curled a little as she said it, as if she were addressing something moldy she'd discovered in her refrigerator.

"So talk."

I could tell she didn't like that. Her narrow face flushed.

"May I come in?"

I didn't know who she was, but I figured, what the hell? I stepped back so she could enter. As soon as the door closed behind her, she was up in my face, waving a nail-chewed finger under my nose.

"I want you to tell me about the murder of Harold Tankersley, and I want to hear it right now. No bullshit, just the facts."

Always cool under pressure, I said, "What?"

"Hank the Tank. You killed him, right?"

"No!" It seemed I was issuing a lot of denials lately. This time, I didn't even know the accuser. "Who the hell are you? You think you can just come in here and start yelling at me?"

"Don't act tough with me, mister. I'm not afraid of you. I've taken on people a lot tougher than you."

I threw my chest out a little. "How do you know how tough I am?"

"I know all about you. You're a two-bit gumshoe who's never handled a big case, who's never even had his name in the local papers."

"I prefer to stay anonymous." Why was I justifying myself to this stranger?

"Well, you're going to get plenty of ink once I nail you for Hank's murder."

That made me step backward.

"Just who the hell are you? And what are you doing in my room?"

She reached inside her linen jacket. My hand snaked behind me before I remembered Romero had taken my gun. She pulled her hand out and offered me a business card. I exhaled loudly, tried to relax, took the card. It said: "Felicia Quattlebaum, Section Editor, *Star News,*" and listed her Florida office address and telephone number.

"So," I said. "A reporter."

"Not a reporter, stupid. An editor. Read the card. I was Hank Tankersley's boss."

It took a second for that to soak in. It was hard to imagine hulking Hank answering to this little peanut of a woman. She didn't seem to notice my difficulty as she barged ahead.

"Any time a reporter gets killed, it gets the media's juices flowing. Before long, reporters from all over the country are going to be knocking on your door. But I'm here to tell you, I'm the one who matters. I'm the one who's going to get the goods on you, and see you go to jail."

I was beginning to get my fill of this.

"Look," I said, checking the card, "Ms. Quattlebaum, I appreciate that you're in a hurry to solve this murder. And, believe me, so am I. But you're barking up the wrong tree. I didn't do it."

"Horseshit. I've talked to the police. You're the prime suspect. The cops may be sitting on their hands, but I'm not. I flew all night to get out to this cowtown while the trail was still warm. I get here, and there's no mystery to it. It's obvious you did it. The question is who paid you and how much?"

Ooh, she had a nasty mouth on her. I huffed and sputtered and finally managed to say, "If somebody had paid me a lot of money to off your reporter, would I still be here?"

I gestured around my room and she seemed to notice it for the first time. Her lip did that disgusted trick again.

"Even you wouldn't be stupid enough to try to run now. The cops are watching you."

"That's exactly right. In fact, there's probably some in the parking lot right now who would gladly come in here and arrest you for trespassing or assault or something."

"I'm not the one who's broken the law."

"Neither am I. I'm a victim here. I found the body, dutifully reported it, and now everybody thinks I killed the jerk."

She got up in my face again. "Hank Tankersley was not a jerk."

The flush on her face told me something and I said, "Sounds like you were more than his boss."

"What do you mean?"

I backed up out of slapping range, and said, "Maybe the reason you're so worked up is because you had the hots for him."

I must've struck a nerve because her voice rose and she looked like she was ready to take a swat at me.

"I did not! He was one of my reporters. It's my job to look after my people and now one of them is dead."

"Yeah, and that's why you burst in here like this and start accusing me? If I was a murderer, why wouldn't I just kill you, too? I think your emotions have gotten the better of you."

She was really steaming now. There was a wall behind me, so I couldn't back up any farther.

"Hank Tankersley was a fine reporter." Her voice went low as she tried to control herself. "I admired him. But that's all."

"Uh-huh. If he was such a great reporter, what was he doing working for a rag like yours?"

"Excuse me?"

"Don't come off all huffy with me. You work for a scandal sheet and so did Hank the Septic Tank. It would be different if this was *The New York Times* we're talking about, but you guys are celebrity snoops. I don't think you're going to find too many people crying over Tankersley's death."

Her expression was murderous.

"We're professional journalists," she said quietly. "We deserve the same respect and First Amendment protection as other journalists."

"Aw, bullshit. You're a bunch of peeping Toms who hide behind the First Amendment while you violate other people. There's such a thing as privacy."

She looked me up and down, like she was surprised that I'd ever considered such a thing.

"First of all," she said after a moment, "you've got a lot of nerve talking about privacy when you're a window peeper yourself. Second, your opinions on journalism are shit. And third, whatever you think of the *Star News* doesn't give you the right to kill one of our reporters."

"I keep telling you, I didn't do it."

"And *I'm* telling *you,* I intend to nail you for Hank's murder whether the police cooperate or not. We're not going to stand by while one of our own is killed."

She was wagging her finger at me again. I hate that. It reminds me of schoolteachers. I'd had enough.

"I tell you what. You take your best shot. I don't care how pissed off you might be, you can't prove me guilty of something I didn't do. This is America."

I don't know where the patriotic note came from, but it didn't work on her.

"Deny it all you want. But you'd better be looking over your shoulder because I'm coming after you."

"Look, that's enough with the threats. Why don't you get the hell out of here before I throw you out?"

She leaned toward me so we were only inches apart.

"Why don't you try it?"

There was something in her voice that told me I'd better not. She was probably one of those tough little women who take karate classes. She'd chop me in the throat or kick me in the balls or something. I felt my scrotum contract at the thought. I didn't need the humiliation of being whipped by a pint-size skirt.

"How about if I just holler to those cops in the parking lot and have them do it?"

That backed her down a little. She stepped back and tugged her jacket around her like she was pulling together her dignity.

"Sure," she said bitterly, "hide behind the police. They'll protect you for now. But once I collect enough evidence against you, they'll be on my side. It's just a matter of time."

I opened my mouth for another denial, but she turned her back to me and headed for the door. When her hand was on the knob, she looked over her shoulder and said, "I know a lot more about what's been going on here than you think."

The door slammed behind her.

It was a full minute before I moved from where she'd backed me to the wall. And it was about that long before I realized Felicia Quattlebaum might know something about Elvis being alive. If Tank had told anyone, wouldn't it have been his editor? I crossed the room and snatched open the door, but there was no sign of her in the parking lot. The undercover car was parked nose-out across the way and two shadowy figures hunched down in the front seat. I closed the door.

I thought about trying to track her down, but dropped the notion almost immediately. Even if she knows more, I decided, she wasn't about to tell it to me. She was convinced I'd been hired to waste her pal. Besides, I didn't like the idea of getting into another argument with the sawed-off little bitch. She was too good at it.

I poured myself a drink and slumped into the big armchair. I needed some time to think clearly about my situation, to decide what to do next. I felt like I'd rushed down a dead-end alley, and now I had my back against the wall while Romero and Morgan and Felicia Quattlebaum and the detectives in the parking lot all closed in on me.

After half an hour or so of getting steadily more depressed, I decided to see if Romero was at his office. The only way to get some of the heat off me was to spread it around. I was going to tell him about my vanished clients. Well, most of it anyway. I still couldn't bring myself to mention Elvis Presley. If I was going to sort out this mess, I needed to be out on the streets, not slapped in a loony bin.

I was on hold for several minutes before Romero came on the line.

"Not another stiff?" he groaned.

"No, no, nothing like that. I'm keeping my nose clean while your boys are watching me."

Romero said nothing, waiting.

"Thought I'd answer those questions about my client y'all were asking last night."

"Your client said it was okay, huh?"

"Not exactly. It seems they've, uh, skipped town."

There was another long silence.

"That doesn't look good for you, Bubba," Romero said finally. "It would be better if we could talk to them."

"You think I don't know that? But I don't have the slightest idea where they went. I thought maybe you folks could run them down."

"Let us do your work for you, huh?"

"Let's just say you have more resources at your command. I've run out of ideas."

"All right, hold on a minute." I wondered briefly whether Romero was getting a pencil or a tape recorder. He came back on the line. "Shoot."

I told him how Buddy had arrived on my doorstep,
how I'd met his boss, a Mr. Aaron, and how they'd hired
me to tail Tankersley. I left out the part about tossing
Tank's room, trying to stay consistent with what I'd told
him before. I told him Buddy had said Mr. Aaron was a
celebrity, but I lied about recognizing him. I also left out
the fact Webster had told me Tank was a tabloid reporter.
I gave him descriptions of Buddy and Elvis and of the tan
Cadillac Seville.

When I was done, he said, "That's it?"

"That's the whole story."

There was a pause, as if Romero was looking back over
his notes.

"You took on a job without knowing the client's names
or addresses, tailing somebody you didn't know. Someone kills him while you're not looking. When you find
the guy dead, you go through all his things, leaving
fingerprints everywhere. The slugs in Tankersley's body
are the same caliber as the gun you carry. Then your
clients disappear."

"Looks bad, doesn't it?"

"I can't believe you'd make so many mistakes. It isn't
like you."

"I know." I tried to sound contrite. How could I
explain that I was a victim of celebrity fever? I couldn't. I
just had to let him think I was an idiot. It was a hard
thing to swallow.

"Have they finished the tests on my gun?"

"No, I haven't heard from them."

"I swear it will come up clean."

"Maybe so, but that won't be enough to get you off the
hook. Not with Morgan anyway. He really took a strong
dislike to you."

"I seem to bring that out in people."

Romero let that go. He said something about getting
an APB out on the Seville, then hung up.

I poured myself a drink and sipped it while I thought

back over what I'd told Romero. I wasn't sure how much of it he'd bought. It was a goofy story, I had to admit. And the omissions had left nearly audible clanks as I'd told it.

My only hope was that the cops could turn up Elvis. Then Romero would understand why I hadn't been able to tell him the whole story, why I knew he wouldn't believe it.

I haven't been inside a church in maybe ten years, but in times of great stress I sometimes revert to my childhood training. I say little prayers to God, even though most of the time I'm not sure such a thing exists. I don't pray out loud. Just little mental pleadings to the cosmos. This seemed to be one of those times. I prayed for the police to receive divine assistance in locating Buddy and Elvis. Then I said "Amen" and tossed back the rest of the whiskey.

13

I still sat on the bed, lost in my troubles, when the phone went off beside me and made me jump. The empty shot glass fired out of my hands and bounced once and rolled across the linoleum.

I snatched up the phone before it could jangle me further and snarled into the mouthpiece: "What?!"

There was a pause, then a woman, sounding very unsurprised, said, "That's an interesting way to answer the phone."

She had a voice like rose petals on velvet, and it pulled me up short.

"Oh, uh, sorry. The phone sort of startled me."

"Then I'm the one who's sorry."

"No, no, it's okay. I just haven't had much luck with telephones lately."

"Well, maybe your luck is about to change."

Something about that purr made it difficult to breathe, but I tried not to let it show. "How's that?"

"Thanks to the phone, you've met me. That might be enough to get you back on good terms with Ma Bell."

It just might.

"Who is this anyway?"

"My name's Bambi Gamble."

"Bambi Gamble?"

"Uh-huh. And I want to talk to you."

"We're talking now."

"No, I want to talk in person." Her voice got even softer, breathy, like a lover whispering secrets. "Face to . . ." She hesitated long enough for a jolt of anticipation to tremble through the phone line. "Face."

A shudder ran over my body, and I whispered back, "When?"

"How about now?"

"How about it?" I gave her my address.

"I'll be there in ten minutes."

The line went dead. I let the receiver droop in my hand, rubbed the smooth plastic against my cheek.

"My, my, my," I said aloud. "Bambi Gamble."

Anybody named Bambi would have to look like a centerfold, I mused. Twisty blond hair and big tits and painted nails and legs to there, all airbrushed smooth as an inflatable sex doll. Big, mascara-ringed eyes cut to the side, so she's smiling right into the camera, making you feel like you walked in on her while she just happened to be vacuuming in the nude.

I grinned and shook my head, amused by my own chauvinism. That was just the kind of sexist thinking that would get me in trouble with a woman. The voices of every feminist I'd ever met lectured in the back of my mind: Just because a person's named Bambi doesn't mean she'll fit some stereotype. I can't assume that every Bambi and Fawn and Bunny and Kitty I meet is going to be some busty airhead.

Just when I'd convinced myself that Bambi would

be as mousy and bookish as Felicia Quattlebaum, she knocked on the door.

I threw open the door and stared down into the cleavage between two mammoth mammaries. Big, beautiful porcelainlike globes pushed and squeezed and underwired until they looked like they would burst from the low neckline of the silky blouse that struggled to contain them. They shadowed an impossibly narrow waist. Designer jeans molded to her round hips and long legs like spray paint. Blond hair draped her shoulders and fell loose in front, nearly covering one of her enormous blue eyes. She had full, soft cheeks and a pert nose and a mouth like an invitation.

This was no pinup girl. This was beyond that. This was the woman of men's dreams, a creation of lust. The kind of woman an artist might paint, a sex fiend might draw, but not the kind who existed in real life. She was the Greek goddess in polished marble, the full-figured comic book heroine, the sexpot on the pinball machine, the lonely sailor's tattoo.

"Hi." She tossed the softly permed mane back over her shoulder. "I'm Bambi."

"Hi. I'm weak in the knees."

"Really? Are you sick?" Like she didn't know the effect she'd had on me, like it had never happened before.

"No, no, nothing like that. In fact, I've never been better. Come in, have a seat."

She left a cloud of musk and lilacs in her wake. In her spiked heels, she was as tall as me, but she folded into the armchair as gracefully as a heron, and looked up at me and blinked. I felt something go boing in my groin, and sat down on the bed before I became too obvious.

Bambi Gamble smiled over at me, the kind of smile that said she'd been waiting for this moment for a long time. I had, too. I just hadn't known it.

"So you're Bubba Mabry." She sighed. "I've heard a lot about you."

I felt flushed and giddy.

"Oh, really? Like what?"

"Like you're the one who found Harold Tankersley's body."

So that's what she was after. Alarms went off in my head, but I tried to ignore them. Who cared why she came? Having her here was worth all the trouble I'd been through. I'd find a corpse a day if it meant getting a woman like this to saunter through my door.

"Yeah, that's me. I'm the one who found him."

She cocked her head and clucked her tongue and tried to look sympathetic. No matter what her expression, her body and her posture exuded sex. It was like seeing Marilyn Monroe on the silver screen. It doesn't matter whether she can act, what she's saying. We just want to look at her and lust.

"That must've been terrible for you."

"It seems like it was, but I'm having trouble remembering it now."

She smiled and batted her eyes and turned on the innocence. It was clear she'd practiced that expression in front of a mirror, but it still made my belly flutter.

"Do the police know who killed him?"

Ask me anything, I thought, talk to me of death, life insurance, economics. Sell me Amway or a subscription to the *Watch Tower*. Just keep talking. That satiny voice was arousing enough to make me understand why those phone sex companies make fortunes.

"Well, so far, they seem to think I did it."

She frowned. Even that expression was luscious.

"I could never believe that. You're not the kind of person who'd kill someone."

"How do you know? You don't know me."

"Maybe not, but I know men—"

I thought, I bet you do.

"And you're not the kind who kills. You look to me to be a lover, not a fighter."

I caught my breath, and said, "Appearances can be deceiving."

"Not always. Some people are absolutely naked when it comes to their personalities."

I wished she'd stop saying things like "lover" and "naked." If she didn't, I was going to need oxygen.

"What about you?" she said. "Do you have any idea who killed him?"

"Oh, I've got some ideas, but I don't have any real clues. Just hunches."

She uncrossed her legs and leaned forward, showing me the breadth of her breasts.

"Tell me your hunches." She made it sound erotic, an invitation to surrender.

I couldn't ignore the alarms any longer. I forced myself to look away from her, to break the spell long enough to think.

"I don't think I'm sure enough about any of my hunches to share them."

I dared a look. She was waiting, and tossed her hair back. Her wet tongue explored her bottom lip.

"Come on," she murmured. "It'll be fun."

I glanced away again. It was easier this time. I was gaining control of the animal lust that hotly coursed through me.

"Let me ask you something first," I said. "Why are you so interested in Harold Tankersley? What's the connection?"

Now it was her turn to sit back and look away.

"Oh, I've known Hank for years."

"In what capacity?"

"We were friends, more or less. Friendly competitors."

"Competitors?"

"Sure. Didn't I mention that on the phone?"

"Nope."

"Oh, how silly of me. I work for the *Celebrity Tattler*. I thought I told you."

"You're a reporter?"

"Uh-huh. I hope you don't think I was trying to mislead you." Innocent again. Big blue eyes and pursed lips.

I rocked to my feet and walked away from her, clearing my head. How could she be a reporter? The reporters I knew were stooped, whiskery drunks with rumpled corduroy jackets and bad attitudes. Or foul-mouthed, swaggering women like Felicia Quattlebaum. Not goddesses like Bambi Gamble.

"Hank and I often covered the same stories." Bambi's voice didn't rise, though now I was across the room from her. Distance did little to lessen the effect she had on me. "So I'm curious about how he got killed."

"And you want to do a story about it."

"Maybe. Depends on what happened. My editors aren't much interested in anything that doesn't have show business attached."

"They'd be interested in this then," I muttered.

"How do you mean?" She perched on the edge of her chair, her hands toying with her knees.

"Oh, uh, you know, Hank the Tank worked on show business stories. I'm sure you'll be able to drum up some connection to whoever he was covering."

"Who was he covering? Do you know?"

"No, I never really got a chance to talk to him."

"How did you happen to find the body?"

She was pumping me good now, and I swallowed and squinted and tried to think.

"I hate to say this. But I don't think I'm going to tell you."

She made a pouty mouth and tilted her head.

"It would mean a lot to me."

"I know. I wish I could. I mean, I'd like to make you happy. But the cops have me under strict orders not to talk to any reporters."

This was a lie, but I needed someone else's authority

to make it stick. I couldn't rely on my own will any-more.

"If I weren't a reporter, would you tell me?"

"I might, under the proper circumstances, but that's sort of beside the point now, isn't it?"

"You could tell me everything, and if it ever comes up you can tell the police you never suspected I worked for the *Celebrity Tattler.*"

"No, I couldn't. I've also got a client to think about." Although God only knows where he might be.

"Who's your client?"

"Can't tell you that either."

She pouted some more, but it wasn't working on me any longer. My brain had wrested control away from my peter. But I still couldn't look right at her and turn her down. My eyes darted around so much I must've looked like Henry, the street crazy, the one pursued up and down Central by imaginary bees.

She stretched to her feet and arched her back and wet her lips.

"I was hoping you'd be more helpful. You seemed so nice on the phone."

"I wish I could. I really do. My hands are tied."

"No, they're not." She smiled. "But they could've been. Anything might've happened."

I shuddered against the disappointment.

She pulled a business card out of the back pocket of her jeans and tossed it on my bed.

"The number of my hotel is on the back," she cooed. "If you change your mind, give me a call. I think there's lots we could talk about."

She touched one red-tipped finger to her lips, blew me a little kiss and left. The instant the door whispered closed behind her I wanted to cry out, to get her back, to at least look at her some more before she walked out of my life. I stood wringing my hands while a car cranked up outside and drove away.

My knees felt trembly, and I slumped onto the bed. I picked up her card and sniffed her scent from it and read the phone number ten or eleven times. It seemed unfair that life could run a woman like that past you without even a pause. But I couldn't give her what she wanted, and she was gone.

I sighed and retrieved the fallen glass and shakily poured myself another drink at the kitchen counter. I held the warm liquor in my mouth for a second before swallowing, like I could disinfect the longing from my soul.

I wandered across the room and opened the drapes and was stunned to find everything unchanged outside. It's that feeling you get when you exit a matinee and it's still daylight out and you're still in the same old town, no longer part of the adventure on the screen. It's always a disappointment, and this felt much worse than that.

The daylight did one thing for me, though. It reminded me how much work I had to do. Bambi Gamble gliding through my life didn't change my predicament. But she sure took my mind off it for a little while.

14

It was harder this time to shake the cops who tailed me. They'd been burned once and were ready for the little maneuvers I pulled. Finally, I turned across two lanes of oncoming traffic on Central and hit the side streets while the undercover car waited for a break in the flow.

I was in an area near the fairgrounds that the cops call the War Zone. Entire blocks are covered by trailer parks filled not with mobile homes, but with rickety recreational vehicles that are permanently occupied. It's a neighborhood of bikers and junkies and hookers and unsuccessful crooks.

I whipped into one of the trailer parks before the cops could catch up with me. Even though it was a sunny Sunday afternoon, the place looked deserted. I eased the Chevy behind one of the trailers, out of sight. I couldn't watch for the undercover car from there, but I wasn't about to get out of the car. A tawny pit bull was tethered to the steel steps of the trailer by a heavy six-foot chain. He snapped his teeth at the Chevy and lunged against the chain with a ferocity that caused the whole trailer to rock. Froth dripped from his jaws, but he didn't make a sound. Some of these losers have their animals' vocal cords severed so they can't bark and disturb the neighbors. The result is a silent alarm that would deter any burglar. It certainly deterred me. I waited five minutes, wincing each time the dog threw himself against the chain, then backed the Chevy out of the drive and turned back toward The Cruise.

There was no sign of the undercover cops as I arrived at the Double Six Motel, and I found myself smiling in spite of my troubles.

The old Hindu woman in the lobby looked nearly as friendly as the pit bull. She tried to ignore the buzzer, but it finally got to be too much for her and she unlocked the glass door.

"What *you* want?"

She obviously remembered me, and not all that fondly. I guess I'd brought a lot of heat down on her employer. Murders are bad for business.

"I want to talk to your boss."

"He not here."

"I'll wait."

"He not coming back."

"Then I'll talk to you."

"Too busy."

"You can spare a minute."

"Too busy. Already talked to police. You go."

I ignored the dark gnarly finger that pointed out the door.

"So what did you tell the police?"

"Go away."

"You told them to go away?"

She began jabbering in her native tongue. She tried to shoo me toward the door, but I didn't shoo. Suddenly, the curtain across the room flung open, and the turbaned owner filled the doorway.

"I thought you said he wasn't here."

The Hindu woman turned back toward her perch in the window. She looked no happier to see the owner than she had been to see me. She clambered onto the stool like a wizened monkey and said something low to the owner, something that sounded like a warning.

The owner threw out his chest and sniffed. He wore a tight-fitting tunic like those Nehru jackets that were popular for twenty minutes in the Sixties. He raised an index finger the size of a cucumber to his cheek and touched the waxed curl of his mustache. I'd somehow forgotten just how huge the man was. I'd have to be even more polite this go-round. I was gunless.

"Good afternoon." He'd never introduced himself, so I didn't have a name. My private investigator's license was in my hand in case he didn't remember. I could tell from his expression that he remembered, and that he, like the Hindu clerk and everybody else, blamed me for all the trouble.

"What do you want here?"

I couldn't get over his British lilt. It was like talking to royalty.

"Well, first, I wanted to apologize for everything that's gone on, and to tell you it wasn't my fault. I know it might look that way, because I was by here before, but I didn't kill that guy in Number Six."

"Apology accepted."

His gaze went over my head to the door, and his scowl suggested I go with it. I took a deep breath and made my play.

"I was hoping to get a little information from you so that I can help put this thing to rest quicker."

"We told everything we know to the police."

"Yeah, well, that's what this lady here said, but the police aren't exactly sharing everything with me at the moment. I thought maybe you wouldn't mind repeating it."

"I would mind."

I knew better than to try a bribe. He'd nearly tossed me out last time. But something else occurred to me.

"I suppose the police have shut off that room."

"Yes they have. And they've given me no indication when I can put it into use again."

"Hmm. That's a shame. It's not your fault that somebody killed that guy. Why should it cost you money?"

"My sentiments exactly."

"I tell you what," I said, skating toward the thin ice, "how about if I pay you for that room while the police have it locked? I feel responsible for all this somehow. Let me make it up to you."

His expression softened ever so slightly.

"I couldn't let you in the room," he said. "The police forbid it."

"No, no, nothing like that. I don't want to go in there. I just thought it would help you out."

He eyed me skeptically, thinking it over.

"What, then, would you want in return?"

"Nothing, nothing at all. Just consider it my way of making up."

Finally, he nodded curtly.

"Very well. The room is twenty-two dollars a day."

My heart sank a little at that, but I took one of Elvis' crisp fifties from my wallet and handed it over.

"That'll cover yesterday and today," I said. "I'll stop by later with the rest."

The turban nodded, and I noticed he tucked the money into his tunic rather than ring it up on the register.

"I suppose that, in exchange, you'd like me to tell you what we told the police."

I lowered my eyelids coyly, and muttered, "Well, only if there's something you think I need to know . . ."

"In fact, you already are aware of nearly all the

information we could dispense. I told you when you were here before."

I nodded and kept my eyes averted.

"But there was one thing. Someone stopped by the room yesterday morning. She saw them."

He gestured to the Hindu woman, who snarled something at him out the side of her mouth. He ignored it.

"It was two men in a Cadillac. She saw the driver disappear around the corner, apparently going to Mr. Tankersley's room. The other man waited in the car."

I didn't ask why she assumed the guy was going to Tank's room rather than to Number Five or Number Seven, which were also out of sight around the corner. I supposed she recognized all the regulars.

"Did she get a good look at them?"

"No."

"And you told the police about this?"

"Of course."

I nodded again, grateful for the information. I mumbled something about how I'd see him soon with the rest of his money, but he knew I was lying. I backed out of there.

Once safely in the Chevy, I wondered why Romero hadn't mentioned the Seville had been seen at the motel. It must've clicked when I told him that was the car my clients drove. Maybe he figured anybody who'd botched things as badly as I had didn't deserve the help. I resented it a little, but could scarcely blame him. I was the main suspect. Romero had already told me more than the rules allowed. I just had to hope that, taken together, the two tips about the Cadillac were enough to get the cops to really hunt for it. I thought about offering another silent prayer, but it seemed greedy to go to the well twice in one day.

Something else occurred to me. The big towelhead had said one guy waited in the Cadillac while the other went to Tank's room. That seemed to confirm Elvis was involved. I'd been harboring some secret hope that Buddy had committed the murders on his own, without Elvis' knowledge, and then had hustled him out of town. Despite all that had happened, I still wanted the King to come away clean.

I talked to a lot of people that afternoon, slipping onto Central long enough to locate familiar faces, asking questions, then disappearing onto the back streets. If the undercover cops caught up to me, I didn't see them.

Only two of the people I questioned did me any good. Both were friends of Rodent's and both charged me for the information. I'd given up on trying to hold on to the money Elvis had paid me. If I didn't chase down my former clients pretty quickly and sort this out, I wouldn't have to worry about rent. The state would be putting me up.

The first greedy tipster was a black pimp everybody calls Stevie Wonder because he keeps his oiled hair pulled back in tight braids with beads on the ends. He plays to the resemblance, wearing wraparound sunglasses day and night. Stevie Wonder isn't much good as a pimp. He's a little squirt who abhors violence, and bigger, meaner pimps are always stealing his girls. Stevie will lure a babe into the trade, work her for a while, then some big Leroy will come in and, zip, Stevie's looking for a new girl. He's a farm club for hookers who want to move into the big leagues.

I hadn't seen much of Stevie lately, and was a little surprised to spot him traveling on foot past the wedding boutiques that line several blocks of Central. Normally, Stevie Wonder travels by Buick Riviera and his pointed shoes rarely touch pavement. Stevie wore a red-and-black outfit with a short jacket like a matador's, providing a contrast to the ivory tuxedos and virgin-white gowns the mannequins modeled in the windows.

No need to repeat here the banter it took to get what I

needed from Stevie Wonder, or to reveal how much it cost. It will suffice to say that he had one tidbit of information that helped me and he made more per minute on the deal than his girls ever did. The information was this: The day before Rodent died, he had been asking around, trying to locate a master key for the Double Six Motel. Stevie swore he hadn't been able to supply one, but assured me Rodent wouldn't have had much trouble running one down. Plenty of duplicates were floating around, he said. The pimps need them in case there's trouble in one of the rooms. Saves kicking in a lot of doors, he'd said, as if he could ever get enough velocity behind his skinny butt to knock one open.

A master key would explain how the killer could've entered Tankersley's room while the big man was squatting on the toilet. But how was Rodent involved? He certainly wasn't the type to try to bump somebody off. My first guess was that he'd supplied the key to Buddy, who, after all, he'd seen following me. But the second tip I got that afternoon threw my assumption into doubt.

It came from a low-level dope dealer named Eugene, whose most distinguishing feature was a walrus mustache that seemed to cover half his pale face. You could never predict Eugene's moods because they depended on which pharmaceuticals he'd consumed. He was partial to coke and speed and his speech pattern showed it. The man could jabber faster than anybody I'd ever heard. You expect someone who talks that fast to be from up north, but Eugene was locally grown like the pot he sold and his voice had the flat twang of the prairie.

I spotted Eugene at dusk coming out of the Frontier Restaurant, a barn-shaped coffee house across Central from the university. The Frontier is one of the few places you can sit all day without being hassled, as long as you nurse a cup of coffee along, and Eugene and other street freaks find it a handy base of operations. I'd parked on Harvard Street, out of sight behind an apartment building, and Eugene and I practically collided on the side-walk.

"Hey," I said, startled, "I was just coming in to look for you."

"S'that right? Well, you came to the right place, here I am. Like I always say, here today, gone tomorrow."

I didn't know what he meant, but then that was often the case. When he was flying, Eugene just needed to talk. It didn't matter whether the rapid-fire jumble of words made any sense.

"What can I do for ya? Looking for a little score? Why don't you step into my office?"

Before I had a chance to interrupt, he'd turned on his booted heel and pushed back through the door of the restaurant. I followed him past the welcoming video games and past several booths before he kicked a chair out from a table and fell onto it.

"Didn't stay gone long," drawled a heavy-set biker at a neighboring table.

"Well, you know me," Eugene said. "Just can't stay away, I love being in here with you boys so much. Sit down, Bubba. Yeah, these boys here, they love to see me coming, they think I'm the floor show in this place. Ain't that right?"

The biker chuckled and shook his head. Eugene sounded like an auctioneer.

"So, Bubba, what's been going on? Haven't seen you around much lately, where you been keeping yourself?"

With Eugene, you just have to sort of jump in and hope he hears you.

"Guess you heard about Rodent," I blurted.

"Yeah, I heard about it, the poor dumb son of a bitch. Guess he crossed the wrong people, somebody sure was pissed, shot three times and thrown in a Dumpster. What a way to go, huh? I always said I wanted to go quick, but not like that. How about you? Naw, I wouldn't want to get thrown in a Dumpster around here, some wino might try to eat you, those bastards think Dumpsters are where you go for fast food."

The biker at the next table laughed. I leaned across the table, braced for Eugene to take a breath.

"I'm trying to solve it." At first, I wasn't sure he'd heard me. Eugene was either running that motormouth of his, or he was thinking about the next thing he was going to say.

"Yeah, I always thought I'd like to go in a fiery car crash, you know, something big that would make the six o'clock news. Did you see the news last night? They hardly mentioned Rodent. I figured he'd be the big story, everybody around here gets so excited about a murder. Hell, all they talked about was some reporter who got killed over at the Double Six. I say the fewer reporters, the better, but Rodent, he was good people, you know?"

Just when I was sure I'd have to repeat myself, he said, "So you're gonna solve it, huh? Somebody paying you to do it, or you just moved by your long friendship with Rodent? Doesn't sound like you, Bubba, you need a client to get your juices flowing."

He had me sized up, I guess. I said, "It's a long story."

"A long story? That's my specialty. Hell, I got a few minutes, sum it up for me, brother."

I opened my mouth, but he continued.

"So you're just asking around, trying to see if anybody knows anything? Well, I don't know much. I hadn't seen Rodent much lately, I don't know where he'd been keeping himself, hanging out with the wrong people, looks like. That's how you end up dead in a Dumpster. Myself, I try to associate only with the finest class of people."

The biker howled at that one and Eugene slipped him a wink.

"So you hadn't seen him?"

"Now, I didn't say that, I said I hadn't seen him around much. But I did happen to see him, just hours before he was killed, I suppose. Yesterday morning, I was going over to his place to see if he needed to buy any, uh, dry goods, if you know what I mean. He'd been doing quite a business during the police crackdown."

Eugene glanced around to see who was listening.

"But he wasn't home. As I was coming back this way, I just happened to see him in a car going the other direction, stopped at that big intersection at Girard. Normally, I don't pay any attention to who's in other cars around me. Shit, I'm watching the road, you know? But this car was worth noticing, it was a hot one. And there was Rodent in the passenger seat, bigger'n life. I remember thinking, boy, you're moving up in the world. I tried to see who was driving, but the sun was wrong on the windshield and I couldn't tell. But it was Rodent in the passenger seat, I'm sure of it. Guess that's the last time I'll ever see him. I'm not much on funerals."

It hadn't even occurred to me that somebody might throw Rodent a funeral, but I let it go. I was more interested in the car.

"This hot car, can you describe it?"

"Describe it? Shit, I could get a boner just thinking about it. One of these days, I'll have me one of those cars, maybe that's what I'll use for my fiery crash, though it would be a shame to wipe out a fine piece of machinery like that just to get on the TV news."

"What kind of car?" I insisted.

"A Porsche. A red Porsche."

15

It took several minutes and a ten-dollar bill to extricate myself from the conversation with Eugene. I hustled through the fading light to the Chevy and found a mimeographed note under my windshield wiper. Here's what it said:

> Dear Asshole:
> This parking area is for tenants only. All other cars will be towed away at the owner's expense. This is your *only warning*.
>
> —The Management

Nice, huh? That's the prevailing attitude around the university campus, which has about half as much parking space as it needs. I crumpled the note and tossed it into a nearby yawning Dumpster. I thought maybe I'd come by here some night and start a fire in that Dumpster, give The Management something else to keep them busy.

I drove too fast going to 2400 Louisiana, chasing my headlights. Traffic was thick around the malls, and by the time I reached the office building, my nerves were frayed. Then I got a stroke of luck, and I felt better immediately. It was about time something went right.

Jerry Finkelman's red Porsche was parked in the nearly empty lot. I don't know what he was doing back at his office on a Sunday evening, but I didn't wonder about it for long. If the Fates were ready to give me a break, I was ready to take it, no questions asked.

My first inclination was to rush up to Finkelman's office and confront him, but I talked myself out of it and decided to watch the building for a while. Perversity moved me to park in the slot Tankersley had occupied for two days. I was busy thinking about how to approach the concert promoter, what exactly I should say, when he exited the building and walked toward the Porsche. I probably would've had time to hustle over to him, but indecision held me up and he was in the car before I made a move. I started the Chevy and followed him into stop-and-go traffic.

The Porsche headed east when it reached I-40, toward the mountains, and I tried to keep up without being spotted.

Finkelman apparently liked to push his luck in traffic —speeding, changing lanes quickly without signaling, hitting the brakes when he was behind someone poking along at the speed limit. I couldn't tell if that was the way he always drove, or if he was trying to shake me, so I hung back as far as I could without losing him. I checked my mirrors to see who might be following me, but who could tell in such traffic? And keeping up with Finkelman was enough of a challenge.

Finkelman slipped off the freeway at the turnoff for Tramway Boulevard and I followed him down the ramp. When he stopped at the red light, I had no choice but to fall in directly behind him. I hoped the glare of my headlights was enough to keep him from recognizing me in his mirror. He turned north on Tramway and continued to drive too fast.

The Sandias are shaped like cresting waves headed west, and Tramway runs along the base of the steep western slope. From Tramway, you can see the whole city stretched out below. The orange lights of Albuquerque twinkled below us, filling the valley, peeking between the expensive houses that dot the foothills. Just as I began to think Finkelman was leading me on a scenic tour, he turned and followed a narrow two-lane road uphill toward Sandia Tram.

Billboards around the city advertise the tram as "The World's Longest Tramway." The tramway's something like two and a half miles from the bottom to the top, with its cables stretching from one steel tower to another, humming along on reels. The cables tow suspended cars the size of buses. The view is great, but the cars sway in the wind and it's a long way down.

Like a lot of Albuquerqueans, I suspect, I'd been on the tram all of once. It was not long after I came to the city and I went with some other burrhead Air Force recruits to ride to the crest. The restaurant that sits at the top of the tram had been packed, so we'd stood out on a wooden observation deck, huddled like cattle against the wind until it was time to ride back down.

There's a restaurant and bar at the bottom of the tram, too, and I found myself hoping that was Finkelman's destination. But I grabbed my jacket out of the back seat, just in case. I loped across the parking lot to catch up with Finkelman, who'd already entered the brightly lit, big-windowed tram terminal.

The entrance on the west side of the building opens onto stairs that angle up to the central lounge where tram passengers wait. Despite the photographs of grinning skiers in bright parkas that line the walls, the place has the feel of a bus station. Gritty, blank tile floors and

steel-edged steps and painted benches worn thin by
countless butts.

Though it had been nearly fifteen years since I'd been
there, I remembered that the bar and a gift shop opened
off the lounge. And there were more exits out the other
side of the building. I had to take a chance on Finkelman
seeing me.

I eased up the stairs, sticking close to one wall. When I
reached a corner in the staircase, I peeked around it,
trying to appear casual. The layout was unchanged from
the way I remembered it. There wasn't much of a crowd
in the lounge; I guessed most people had ridden up in
time for the sunset. One couple necked on a bench in a
corner, labeling themselves as honeymooners. Two
college-age couples stood close, chatting, showing off
their early tans in short pants they'd regret on the crest.
Another foursome stood nearby for contrast. They were
doughy senior citizens in Ban-lon shirts and muumuus,
lining up for another Sun Belt attraction. The men's
red-veined noses already glowed from drink.

Finkelman stood off by himself, his back to me as he
looked up at the dark mountains through floor-to-ceil-
ing windows. He wore a navy-blue satin baseball jacket
with CREATIVE ENTERTAINMENT scrolled across the back in
white. Everybody wants to look like a rock star. Especially sleazoid promoters who think it might help them get
laid. If Finkelman was worried about being followed, he
didn't show it. He never looked over his shoulder to
where I stood on the stairs.

A very bored brunette behind a counter announced the
tram was departing and a teenager in a jacket that said
"Sandia Peak Tram" threw open the glass doors and led
Finkelman and the others out onto the concrete catwalk
to the waiting tram car. Standing there in my jacket that
didn't say anything, I felt helpless. I certainly couldn't get
on the tram with Finkelman. No place to hide in the big
open car, not even any seats to duck behind. I heard the

124

tram door slam and the big reels groan as the car began
its ascent.

I climbed the rest of the stairs and approached the
counter as the brunette erased grease-pencil marks on a
waxy board behind her and changed the time under the
words "Next Tram Leaves At:" to read fifteen minutes
later. I paid her nearly ten bucks for a round-trip ticket
after she needlessly informed me that I'd just missed the
latest departure. I thumbed through my wallet as I sat on
an empty bench. It had been an expensive afternoon. I
needed to replenish my supply from the dwindling Elvis
funds locked in my room.

I caught myself muttering a couple of times while I
waited on the bench. It's a bad habit to fall into, but I
couldn't seem to help myself. There was so much on my
mind. I had to ask myself what I was doing here, waiting
for the tram like a tourist so I could ride to the top to find
out Finkelman is having a quiet dinner alone. If that
was the case, maybe I'd join him. I'd like a few minutes of
his time, time enough to ask about Rodent and what
Finkelman might know about motel keys. At the top of
the mountain, I'd have at least fifteen minutes while he
waited for the next tram down.

It was closer to thirty minutes before my ride departed. During the wait, a few other passengers drifted in
and busied themselves with not staring at each other.
One young woman looked nervously up at the mountains
through the windows the whole time, giggling to her date
about her fear of heights. I made a mental note not to
stand near them in the tram.

There wasn't much wind, so it was a smooth ride. Even
though we moved more or less horizontally, it felt
somehow like an elevator as the tram car glided on its
cables. I stood near the eastern windows, paying more
attention to what awaited at the top than to the lights of
the city that had most of the passengers enraptured in the
other end of the car. Darkness below us disguised what

a long drop it would be, and even the nervous Nellie I'd overheard earlier seemed to forget her fears. The downbound tram passed us with a whoosh at the halfway mark. I tried to see whether Finkelman was inside, but who could tell? That gave me something else to worry about. We docked with a bump at the crest terminal and were bathed in light as we disembarked. Keeping my eyes open for Finkelman, I stuck close to the other passengers as they clumped along the broad boardwalk toward the High Finance restaurant.

Some bristly pine trees grow alongside the walk, and I dropped into their shadows as the others continued to the restaurant entrance. The mile's difference in altitude made my breath short and I felt disoriented as I tried to remember the layout of the place. Bright globes of light burned here and there, making the sidewalk and observation deck too visible from the windows that lined the wall of the restaurant. Still, nothing was being accomplished by standing where I couldn't see inside.

I turned up my jacket collar and strolled along the boardwalk toward the observation deck. City lights glowed below like spilled Mardi Gras beads, but my attention was on the diners who sat on the other side of the thick windows, munching on their salads and sipping their wine. My stomach growled to remind me of how long it had been since I'd eaten, but I tried to ignore it.

When I'd made my way halfway around the circular building, I spotted Finkelman's jacket blaring at me. He sat by the window at a table for two. Across from him, stretching his mouth around a sandwich, was Buddy, his eyes closed in gastronomical bliss. He wore a dark suit that barely stretched around his bulges and his gold pinkie ring winked at me as I recognized him. I threw up an arm and made as if I was scratching the back of my head, hoping my sleeve threw enough of a shadow on my face. I hurried across to the darkest part of the deck and leaned against the smooth wooden rail. Just another blue-jeaned tourist, staring out at the view.

From that vantage point, I could see both men in profile as they leaned across the table. Finkelman wasn't eating, but a drink sat at his elbow. He looked angry and his lips were flapping very fast, as if trying to persuade Buddy of something. Buddy seemed more interested in the food he was knocking down in record time. His jowls jiggled when he chewed.

I thought longingly of my Polaroid, safely locked away in my room. Wouldn't Elvis be interested in a photo of his sidekick dining with a concert promoter? Of course, I'd have to find Elvis to show it to him, so it might not have done me much good.

About the time I was beginning to feel the thin-air chill in my bones, Finkelman suddenly got up from the table and stalked away toward the entrance on the far side of the restaurant. Buddy seemed unperturbed, and continued eating.

My feet twitched, trying to follow Finkelman out of habit, but I convinced them otherwise. There was no question about which man I should tail. Buddy could lead me to Elvis. I didn't know what their connection to Finkelman might be, but they, not the promoter, were the ones who could solve my problems.

If Buddy went to the tram, there was no way I could follow undetected. But I could grab him and make enough of a commotion to get somebody to call the cops. From there, it would be a simple matter to turn him over to Romero. Then again, how quickly could the cops get to the mountaintop? Without a gun, how could I hold the fat slob long enough? He could disappear into the dark forest that sloped away in three directions. I suddenly got a sense of the unseen precipice at my back, a touch of vertigo that made me grasp the handrail.

Buddy signaled a waitress and gave her a handful of

cash. He wiped his mouth, took a last slug from his Budweiser, wiped again and stood up. I tried to shrink farther into the shadows and turned my back on the building, knowing it would be human nature to check the view a final time. But Buddy seemed oblivious as he turned away and went the opposite direction from the entrance, picking his way between tables. He disappeared around a corner, and I figured he was going to take a leak. But I heard a back door open and close and heavy steps on the boardwalk. Then I spotted Buddy in the lights outside the restaurant, walking away toward the forest. I slipped over to the cover of the building and eased around it with my back practically pressed to the windows, drawing stares from the diners inside.

A flashlight flicked on up ahead, throwing Buddy's bulky body into silhouette. The light bounced as he stepped off the boardwalk and onto a rocky path that led away through the woods. The path he was on, I knew, is part of a network of trails that laces the mountaintop. This one runs more than a mile, connecting the tram and restaurant to an overlook that's the end of a highway that runs up the backside of the Sandias. You can't drive to the High Finance restaurant, but you can hike over from the overlook. Buddy, it seemed, was hiking back.

I wished for the flashlight in my glove compartment, so impossibly remote from where I stood. There was no choice but to follow him, stumbling along in the dark, and to hope Elvis waited at the overlook parking lot.

Lord knows I tried to be quiet. But jagged rocks erupted here and there on the trail and pine branches swatted me in the face and twigs crunched underfoot. Moonlight helped some, but pines and aspens shaded the trail most of the way and I soon found it was easier to walk by feel than by sight. I kept my eyes on the bobbing flashlight up ahead. It disappeared from time to time as the trail twisted through the trees, but always reappeared, giving me a target to pursue. I fell twice, tripping over roots and rocks, but managed to catch myself with only minor scrapes both times. At one point, I found myself mumbling aloud about the folly of following through the forest and told myself to shut up before Buddy heard. Probably no danger of that, though. He was making much better time than I could, and the light seemed more distant every time I spotted it.

Desperation hurried me as I crossed an open meadow instead of sticking close to the trees. The trail looked like a black snake as it wound across the field, shadowed by grass and thorny shrubs that grew along it. Buddy's light had disappeared into the dark forest on the far side and I knew it couldn't be much farther to the parking lot. It seemed as if I'd been fumbling along for miles.

The trees swallowed me up again, but the trail went suddenly smoother and wider, some sort of old dirt road, and I could make better time. The flashlight was nowhere to be seen. I geared up to a sort of lumbering lope. My lungs shrank against the thin air and I felt lightheaded almost immediately, but I plunged ahead. I topped a rise in the trail and could see the lights of the parking lot looming ahead. I had spots before my eyes from oxygen deprivation and I slowed. Buddy was nowhere. My breath was coming in gasps and I felt very much like I needed to sit down, but I forced myself to keep up my stiff-legged gait, trying to reach the parking lot before Buddy could drive away.

Then a voice splintered the night: "Thtop right there."

I stopped, grateful for the chance to catch my breath. I reeled about in the middle of the wide trail before I got my hands gripping my thighs and stood still, drinking in air. Buddy appeared from between two shadowy trees and flicked his flashlight on me. I must've looked like a possum in the headlights, my mouth hanging open and my eyes wide.

"Thtand up thtraight," he said. "Put your handth up."

My lungs didn't like that idea. The rawness there made

me want to press my elbows to my body. But I managed to get my hands up there and hold them. Buddy stepped closer and I could make out the pistol in his hand. It suddenly didn't seem so hard to keep my hands up. They seemed to float up there on their own accord.

Between gasps, I said, "I want . . . to talk . . . to you."

"Thut up."

If my hands went any higher, they'd lift me off the ground.

Buddy seemed to study me for a long time. His face was in shadow behind the flashlight glare, and I couldn't tell what he was thinking. Finally, he said, "My, my, Bubba, you thouldn't be following me. What are we going to do with you?"

I had a pretty good idea, but I said, "I just want to talk. You boys have left me in a world of hurt. The cops think I killed that reporter."

There was a pause, then he said calmly, "Didn't you?"

That straightened my spine.

"You know damned well I didn't."

"All I know ith that we're out of here. We're gone. And you can't follow uth. I'll do whatever it taketh to thtop you."

He reached forward with the gun, like he was going to touch my chest with it. A car horn sounded in the parking lot, shattering the forest silence before the pistol could. Buddy's head jerked toward the sound, and I brought both my fists down on top of his skull.

The blow staggered him and I grabbed for his gun with both hands. I got hold of it, but he was surprisingly strong as he tried to wrestle the barrel toward me. I hip-checked him, but the blow was absorbed by layers of fat and he didn't even grunt. He brought the flashlight down on my head, which stung, but it was plastic and didn't do the trick and I held on to the gun hand.

Buddy pulled the trigger and the gun went instantly hot in my hands. I didn't know if I was shot, but I was so surprised that I jumped back and threw up my hands. My bony elbow caught Buddy on the tip of the nose and his head snapped back and he yelped. The gun went off again, but it was pointed at the ground. I crashed my wrist down onto his, and he dropped the gun. I tried to grab him in a bear hug, but my arms just slid around on his polyester-slick fatness. It was like trying to wrestle a peeled banana.

I stepped back to try a different tactic and he sank a fist into my stomach. I wasn't ready for it and it lifted me up on my toes. I must've doubled over from the force of it because the butt of the flashlight came down on the back of my neck. Then I was on my knees with dirt in my mouth, hearing Buddy's feet pounding away toward the parking lot. The flashlight beam swung back and forth as he puffed away. I tried to get up off my knees, but all my joints felt rubbery.

A car engine roared to life in the parking lot and tires squealed as it took off. I slowly clambered to my feet. Another engine cranked up and I saw a dark Ford Escort pass under the halogen lights that ringed the parking lot. I could see another car or two parked in the lot, probably belonging to teens whose necking had been spoiled by nearby gunshots. I thought about comandeering one of the vehicles to set off after Buddy, but it was too late. Then I remembered the gun, and I felt around with my feet until I found it.

The gun's heft felt familiar. I ran my hands over it and it dawned on me that it was exactly like my Smith & Wesson, the one Romero had confiscated. What a horrible coincidence. No two guns fired the same, I knew, and the ballistics tests still should be my salvation. But if this was the gun that killed Tankersley and Rodent, wouldn't the cops find it hinky that the murder weapon was the model that happened to be my personal favorite? And now it had my fingerprints all over it.

Nevertheless, I carried the gun through the woods

with me on my way back to the tram. Without Buddy's flashlight as a beacon, it would be easy to stumble off the trail and get lost. There were bears in these mountains.

I didn't see any bears, though something skittering through dry leaves made me jump once. The trail was more familiar now, and the going was easier because I didn't have to worry about stealth. Once I could see the lights of the restaurant, I ducked off the trail long enough to ditch the pistol. I wiped the prints off it with my shirttail, then buried it under some leaves at the base of a tree. I wasn't sure I'd be able to find it again, but I knew enough about its location that Romero's people could turn it up later. I just had to think of a convincing way to tell him how I knew it was there. It might look to them like I just went to the mountaintop to hide the gun and invented the rest. Unless Finkelman could lead the cops to Buddy, I still had no proof he existed. I felt sure nobody had witnessed our struggle in the woods, which, considering how it had turned out, was probably just as well.

16

When I got home, the tape on my message machine was filled up. That had never happened before. I had time for a drink while the thing rewound.

Most of the messages were from reporters—both local papers, all three TV stations, plus two of the networks; *The National Enquirer,* The Associated Press and somebody from *People* magazine. A couple of them had been cut off by my temperamental machine and had been forced to call back to finish leaving their names and numbers. I didn't write any of them down.

The one message that concerned me was from Steve Romero. It went like this:

"Bubba, this is Romero. Captain Morgan is upset because you keep disappearing on us. He wants a meeting. Call me soon as you get home."

No joking around, no friendly chuckle. And "a meeting" with the head of Homicide. Visions of torture danced through my head. Electric wires, lead pipes, hot cigarettes, dental work.

Well, I thought, there's no way I'm calling them tonight. I need some rest. If they want me, they can come and get me. I scavenged through my sparse pantry for some dinner, then turned out the lights and flopped onto the bed with my clothes on to think it all over.

Finkelman clearly knew Buddy, which led me to believe he knew about Elvis. He might even know their whereabouts, but I didn't know his whereabouts and didn't have the energy to do anything about it if I had. The tussle with Buddy had taken a lot out of me. I had a purple bruise on the back of my neck that made it hard to get comfortable.

Buddy obviously had told Finkelman something he didn't like. The little promoter had been hopping mad. Maybe he told him that he killed Tank and Rodent. That would be enough to set Finkelman off. But what was Finkelman's connection? Was he trying to take Elvis public again? The King looked pretty good for a guy his age, fit and drug-free, maybe ready to tour. Maybe he was lonely for the public's attention and was looking for a way to return. Finkelman certainly had ticked off the financial benefits with ease. Like he'd thought about them before.

My second drink went right to my head, and I dozed off and dreamed of Bambi Gamble's hooters. I'd been asleep maybe an hour or two, when someone banged on my door. I'd been expecting the police and was still dressed. I smoothed down my hair on my way to the door.

Felicia Quattlebaum burst into the room.

"Good, you're still up," she said brusquely, ignoring the mussed bedcovers. "I need to talk to you."

I flicked on the overhead light and she settled into my armchair. Her feet barely reached the floor. She looked excited about something, her eyes shining, but she didn't seem as angry as she'd been at our first encounter. I kept my distance.

She must've sensed my hesitation because she began by saying, "I guess I, um, uh, owe you an apology for busting in here and accusing you before."

Apologies are like praise; I hear them so rarely I never know how to react. I said something along the lines of "Shucks" but she didn't seem to notice.

"I never really believed you were guilty, but I had to come on strong to see if I could shake anything loose."

She wore a hip-length cardigan of navy blue, and she produced a pack of cigarettes from its pocket and said, "Mind if I smoke?"

I shook my head, and immediately regretted it. I haven't had a cigarette in five years, but the smell of one in my room would have me craving tobacco for days. She shook one free of the pack and lit it, all in smooth, well-practiced motions. She blew out a puff of smoke and leaned back in the chair, looking at me. I sat on the end of the bed, still not knowing exactly how to take her.

"Don't you see?" she said. "You were the obvious choice. You're not exactly the most well-respected private eye in town, yet Elvis picked you to do his dirty work."

Elvis! She'd said the name! She knew! My eyes must've goggled and my mouth fell open.

"That's right. I know all about it. I'm the only one Hank told."

I jumped to my feet for no reason, then tried to pace while I absorbed the news. My room's not laid out for pacing—the bed's in the way—so it must've looked as if I was wandering aimlessly. Maybe I was.

"You've known all along."

She nodded. It looked like she was trying not to smile. She hid behind her cigarette, puffing smoke like a train.

"You can get me off the hook with the cops!"

She didn't nod this time. She cocked her head to one side, like she wanted to nod, but had one condition. It's the gesture of a true dealmaker, a player, and I didn't like it one bit.

"What?"

"What what?"

"What's that look? You're going to tell the cops all about Elvis, and get me off the hook. Right?"

I must've looked menacing, towering over her with my fists clenched, but she just blinked at me.

"Well," she said, blowing out smoke, "you can haul me down to the police station and I'll tell them everything I know."

I exhaled loudly, tried to get a grip on myself.

"Or you can take them the genuine item."

I sat down again. "You know where I can find him?"

She nodded and let the smile slip to the surface. She looked pretty when she smiled, in a bookwormish sort of way.

"I didn't know until tonight."

"What happened tonight?"

"I followed his sidekick to their hideout. It's over on the other side of the mountains. A place called Tijeras?"

She mispronounced the "j" as a "j" instead of an "h," but I let it pass. She was new in town. And I didn't want to interrupt.

"It's on a dirt road, but I wrote down the directions on my way out, so we can find it again."

She snuffed out her butt in the tinfoil ashtray the maid insists on leaving in my room every week. She looked up at me with amusement in her eyes and said, "Want me to take you over there?"

I snatched up my jacket and said, "If you're waiting on me, you're late."

Outside, as I locked up my room, she said, "Your car or mine?"

I turned to find a dark blue Escort parked next to my car.

"You were on top of the mountain," I said, finally putting it together.

"Uh-huh." She looked suddenly impatient, like I should be quicker on the uptake. Like I hadn't just rolled out of bed.

"That was you who honked the horn."

She nodded. "Which car?"

"Let's take mine. That little thing of yours wouldn't have enough horsepower to keep up with them."

"I did okay in the mountains."

I unlocked the door for her and walked around to the driver's side while she hefted a camera bag out of her car. After I slid behind the wheel, I said, "What were you doing up there anyway?"

Enough light spilled from the windows of my room that I could see her face. She grinned at me.

"I'd been following you, thinking you'd lead me to Elvis," she said. "When you went up the tram, I had to think of something else. I'm scared of heights."

She looked away, out the window, as she said it. I didn't touch it. People are afraid of things. With me, it's snakes and cops and lawyers, which I sort of lump together. With her, it's heights. Fine.

"I saw on the map that you could drive up the other side of the mountains, so I drove around there, following the signs. I didn't realize that the road and the tramway don't connect. I was sitting in the parking lot, trying to figure out what to do next, when I saw a flashlight coming up the trail. Fortunately for you, I waited around to see who it was."

"How could you tell it was me?"

"Despite the glasses, I've got great night vision. Besides, who else would be having a shootout on top of the mountain?"

She had me there, but I said something about it being the Wild West and let her continue. I wanted the rest of the story.

"When I saw that little fat guy come running out of there, I figured he must be Elvis' sidekick, the one Hank told me about. So I followed him."

"What about me? I could've been dying up there."

"I saw you get to your feet. Besides, you weren't the story anymore. The other guy was."

"Buddy," I said.

"What?"

"His name's Buddy, or at least that's what he goes by."

By this time we're on San Mateo, roaring toward I-40. It's a long way to Tijeras, and I didn't want Elvis slipping through my fingers.

"That fits with what Hank told me."

"What else did he tell you?"

She clammed up, and I could feel her looking at me. Finally, she said, "I guess there wouldn't be any harm in pooling our information. You're not likely to get it into print before I could."

"I'm not likely to get it into print at all. I don't want to go public with this thing. I just want to deliver Elvis to the cops and let them sort it out. No headlines for me."

She sort of cooed, which surprised me. "Don't you want to be in *my* story?"

"No way. Promise me you'll forget you ever met me."

"I don't know if I can do that."

I wasn't sure what she meant, but I didn't want to argue any more. I wanted to hear the rest of what she'd learned from Tankersley.

"Okay, here's what happened," she began. "Hank was in Phoenix working on a story about a celebrity fat farm when he spotted a guy who looked just like Elvis Presley coming out of a drugstore. Hank didn't really think it was him, but he was having a slow afternoon, so he followed the guy out to this big house in the desert. The guy obviously had money, so Hank's thinking maybe there's a feature here on some eccentric millionaire Elvis impersonator. He tries to get some information about the guy and comes up dry everywhere.

"Finally, he goes to the guy's house, where he'd followed him that first day, and your fat friend makes some threats and runs him off with a pistol."

Traffic was light on the freeway and we were making good time.

"Well, that just got Hank more curious. That's the way he was." She paused for a moment out of respect. I didn't look over at her.

"Once Elvis found out Hank was on to him, he and Buddy left town immediately. It was beginning to look more and more to Hank like the guy really was Elvis, living undercover. Like all those reported sightings we'd printed since Elvis died weren't so crazy after all. So he tracked him to Albuquerque, and you know the rest."

I nodded, picking up my cue, and told her what had happened once I was hired by Buddy. I left out a few things—tossing Tank's room, the Finkelman connection, Bambi Gamble—to keep my story consistent with what I'd told the cops and to keep a hole card or two. By the time I finished, we'd entered steep-walled Tijeras Canyon and it was time to start consulting her directions.

"So who was the guy in the red Porsche?" she asked.

"What's that?"

"The guy you were following while I was following you."

"I can't get over the fact that you were shadowing me. I never caught on to you."

"I'm good at it."

She lit another cigarette. She opened her window a crack to let out the smoke, and the air that rushed in was cool and sweet. We'd turned off onto a two-lane blacktop road that twisted through hills covered by a pygmy forest of piñon and juniper. The dark sharp-cornered shadows of houses on the hilltops showed here and there against the star-littered sky.

"Your turn's coming up on the right," she said. "Who was the guy in the Porsche?"

"Jerry Finkelman. He's a friend of Buddy's. But I didn't know that for sure until I saw them together on top of the mountain."

"Turn here."

I kept going straight, and her voice rose. "I said turn. Turn! You missed your turn. Jesus."

I cut the lights once I was well past the dirt road, stopped the car and backed up until I could make out the turnoff in the moonlight. I eased the car through the turn, between the shadowy ditches, and let it bump slowly up the road. Felicia Quattlebaum huffed, but I knew I'd made my point about who was the private eye here.

When she next spoke, it was in a whisper to show me how close we were. "It's the third left."

The houses at the end of the first two driveways had lights on inside and out, but the third one was dark and discouraging.

I drove on past, turned around, then parked facing the driveway, as close as possible to the junipers that lined the dirt road. The driveway was tucked into an arroyo between two hills and we were on high ground beyond it, hopefully unnoticeable. I cut the engine.

"Okay, look," I said, "I'm going to check out the house. You stay here and keep an eye out."

"No way, buster."

"What?"

"I'm going with you."

"No, you stay here and keep an eye out. I'll go check out the house."

"I said I'm going."

"Look at the house. There's nobody home. I'm just going to look around real quick, then I'll be right back. You stay here."

It was like talking to Tarzan. You stay. Me go.

"Listen, Bubba, I'm the one who found this place and

I'm not going to take any chances on you screwing up my story. Clear?"

So that was it. She thought I'd screw it up. She'd seen Buddy get the best of me in the forest (he had a gun!) and now felt I couldn't handle the job. My manhood had been challenged. I carelessly slammed the door and stomped off through the piñons. Pretty soon, I could hear her scurrying along in back of me, making little grunting noises as she lugged her camera bag through the snatching trees. I spotted some cholla cactuses and the sight made me smile with anticipated revenge.

The sinuous limbs of the cactuses' shadow made me think for the first time of snakes. I told myself it was cool enough that all the rattlers would be safely inactive in their burrows, but I still watched my step. It didn't help to have Felicia Quattlebaum rattling around behind me. Finally, I stopped and let her catch up and we stalked silently side by side, determined as two hungry hunters.

The flat-roofed adobe was empty and locked up tight. We futilely tried to peer through draped windows. I judged that the double-bolted doors would take approximately the rest of my life to pick.

I figured Buddy had spotted Felicia following earlier and they'd disappeared again, but I said, "Let's wait in the car. We'll walk down the driveway. If anybody comes, dive into the trees."

17

So," I said after we'd settled in the Chevy, "tell me about yourself."

"What?"

"Tell me about yourself. We're going to be stuck out here on surveillance for a while. Might as well get to know each other."

"Why?"

She was still steamed about the chase through the cactuses.

"It'll help pass the time."

"Oh." She thought it over. "Okay, what do you want to know?"

"Well, start with telling me where you're from."

"Indiana."

"But you live in Florida now."

"Yes."

"I've never been there. It must be nice."

"It's too humid."

"I know what you mean. That's why I live out here."

"So what else do you want to know?"

I could tell this wasn't going to be easy. Some people have no sense of idle chitchat. People from the South understand the pleasures of just sitting and talking. One person tells a story or makes an observation. The other person says, "I know what you mean, brother. The same thing happened to me . . ." Then he relates a story of his own. Then it's somebody else's turn. It doesn't matter much if the stories are truly related, as long as something in what the other person said made you think of it. Then you can say, "Same thing happened to my Uncle Jimmy . . ." That's the way you get to know people, the way you learn how much we all have in common.

I realize now Felicia Quattlebaum was uncomfortable with my probing. She was the one who usually asked the questions. But at the time I barged ahead, determined to keep her talking. I needed all the help I could get staying awake. It was her fool idea to come out here to the middle of nowhere in the middle of the night. She could at least talk.

By the time I'd heard her life story (the central theme of which was her transformation from award-winning reporter on her hometown paper to high-paid, celebrity-hunting pit bull for the *Star News*), one bit at a time, I was worn out from asking so many questions. When it became clear I was giving out, she mercifully said, "What about you? Where are you from?"

I gave her the short version, and didn't mention the Cutwallers or that my mother might have once graced the pages of the *Star News* in her role as the Jesus Lady from Nazareth, Mississippi.

Felicia Quattlebaum *acted* interested, at least. I mean, she wasn't exactly taking notes, but she was giving me those little "hmm-mms" that mean "please continue." I guess that, too, comes automatically to reporters, but it was enough to keep me talking freely. I don't need much encouragement.

I felt myself warming to her a little. Not because of anything overt that she did. She just sat there, puffing on her cigarettes and coolly watching my silhouette as I gestured my way through the anecdotes that more or less make up my biography. The time I was snakebit when I was fourteen (sick for a week, but survived). Joining the Air Force and moving west. The lackadaisical way I'd decided to become a private eye.

Even though I had no respect for her line of work, it sounded like she was a success in it, and that made me defensive. I tried to make my investigations sound exciting, but it came off a little forced. I felt my ears burning, and I thwarted the blush by going right to the point.

"What about that anyway? You obviously don't think much of private detectives. How come you came back and got me when you found this house?"

I'd caught her off-guard, and it took her a second to answer.

"Once I saw you fight with Buddy on the mountain, I could be sure you weren't on their side. Or at least weren't anymore. I was pretty sure all along you weren't the one who killed Hank. But you were the only one I'd located. That's why I followed you. Once I saw Buddy pull a gun on you, I thought you'd want to help me expose them."

"But if all you want is the story, you could've stayed out here yourself and staked these guys out."

"I feel more comfortable when I have someone with me who knows the lay of the land. Look at what happened earlier. I went up that highway to the crest without realizing it wouldn't take me where I wanted to go."

"Lucky for me."

She patted my arm, an awkward sort of gesture that said enough with the gratitude already. Her hand was soft against my skin and her touch made something vibrate in my arm. It was the first show of a tender side, and I had to blow it by shooting my mouth off.

"It occurs to me that having me on surveillance with you is one way to keep an eye on me while you watch for them. You can't be in two places at once, so you bring me along."

She turned away, glared out the window, pissed again. Now that we'd gotten along for a few minutes, it seemed important to keep her happy. It sure made things less tense in the car.

"Not that it matters. I appreciate being brought along, no matter what you were thinking. I've got a lot to lose if these guys get away, a lot more than a newspaper story, and I'd hate to be sitting on the sidelines."

She relaxed a little, but didn't look over at me. I scrambled around for something else to say.

"Guess everybody wants this story. I had so many calls from reporters today that they filled up the tape on my message machine."

She turned to me, a little alarmed. "You didn't talk to any of them?"

"No, no, no. I just erased the tape. Oh, well, I did talk to one who came by my place."

"What did you tell him?"

"Her. It was definitely a her. And I didn't tell her anything."

Felicia stiffened.

"What was her name?"

"Uh, I think it was Bambi. Bambi Gamble."

She twisted in her seat like she was ready to whop me. I flinched.

"You talked to Bambi Gamble?"

"Yeah. You know her?"

"Oh, I know her. You can count on that, bub."

"It's Bubba."

She ignored me, too caught up in her rant. "Bambi Gamble is the worst kind of reporter. A story pirate. She follows other reporters around, figures out what they're up to, then beats them into print with their own story. She's one bitch who'll do anything for a story."

"Sounds like you don't like her much."

"I could kill her without batting an eye."

That chilled things in the car. I was afraid to say anything else. After a moment, Felicia continued, her voice low and murderous.

"I had a reporter, guy named Phil, who'd gotten on to a big story about Roseanne Barr. This was early, before everybody did Roseanne into the ground. We were all set to go to press with it when Phil just happened to run into Bambi Gamble in a bar. The next morning, Phil wakes up in a strange hotel room with a hangover and a sore back. Our story was in the *Celebrity Tattler* two days before we could get it into print."

I said nothing. The windows were fogging with the heat she generated.

"Phil knew better. He knew Bambi's reputation. We fired him. But he said it was worth it to spend a night with her."

I knew exactly what Phil meant.

"Well, she tried some of that stuff with me," I said. "But it didn't work. I didn't tell her anything."

"Are you sure? Maybe you let something slip."

"I guess I'd know if I had."

"I'm not so sure. Bambi Gamble has a way of clouding men's brains."

"She certainly does."

I thought I heard Felicia's teeth grind.

"Did she know about Elvis?"

"No. At least, she didn't say anything about him."

There was a long silence while Felicia steamed. I groped around for another topic and came up with the one thing that would piss her off even worse. How was I to know?

"What kind of name is that?" I asked. "Quattle-baum?"

Even in the darkness, I could see the hard glint in her eyes.

"What's it to you?"

"Uh, nothing. Just curious."

"Keep your curiosity to yourself. Okay?"

"Jeez, I was just trying to change the subject. What are you so worked up about?"

"Oh, right, you wouldn't see it, would you, Bubba?" She sort of spat my name at me. "You didn't grow up with other kids calling you Fellatio Quacklebutt. Or worse."

I couldn't think of anything worse than Fellatio Quacklebutt, but I know kids can be cruel.

"That's terrible. I never considered what a burden a name could be. People have always just called me Bubba."

"Believe me, you're lucky. Even something as dumb as Bubba is better than some odd fucking name that people can't leave alone."

I'd never really thought of my nickname as being dumb, and I think I resented the characterization. But maybe it made us even. Once again, it seemed prudent to change the subject.

"Do you really believe this guy is Elvis Presley?" I asked.

She shrugged and huffed and scrunched down in her seat.

"I don't know. I believe that Hank believed it, and that was good enough for me when I told him to follow them. Hank had great instincts about such things. But now he's dead, and I think I'm going to have to see Elvis with my own eyes before I can believe it a hundred percent."

"Mm-hmm," I said noncommittally. Nobody wanted to come right out and say they believed it. It required a

leap of faith, something a person might be able to do if
Jesus appeared in a kitchen or something like that. But
believing in Elvis seemed silly. I didn't want to say
anything else about it, but she forced the issue.

"You've seen him. What do you think?"

"I, uh, think it's a tremendous resemblance. The guy
really does look the way Elvis would look if he hadn't
died, if he'd cleaned up his act and started exercising. He
looks like he's in good shape."

"But you don't think it's really him."

"Well, I just can't bring myself to believe it, you know?
The man's been dead seventeen years. But let me put it
this way: I can see why Tankersley would believe it's him.
The resemblance is strong, and the guy really is living on
the run. If he's not Elvis, he's sure pretending to be."

There was a pause, then I said, "Guess it would be a
better story if it's him, huh?"

"It's a pretty damned good story either way. The
murder of a reporter. Someone who's at least *pretending*
to be a dead rock star."

That edge was back in her voice. I could tell she
wanted it to be Elvis, if for no other reason than to prove
Tankersley was correct in his final pursuit. My waffling
didn't help matters.

"Well," I said, "I hope for your sake that it's him. As
for me, as long as I can find the guys who hired me and
turn them over to the police, I'll be happy. I don't care
who they are."

She shifted in the seat so she was facing me.

"You're not going to want to turn them in immediately, are you? I want to interview them first, take photos."

"And how do you expect to manage that?"

"You can keep them covered while I talk to them. It'll
take the police forever to find this place. I'll have time."

"Keep them covered? With what? I don't have a gun."

The news floored her. She took a minute to gather

herself, sighed heavily over my ineptitude and said, "A private eye without a gun?"

"The cops took it. I only have the one gun. It's not like I can afford an arsenal. Or need one."

"You don't just go out on a stakeout unarmed, do you?"

"Sometimes," I said defensively. I hated the trace of a whine in my voice.

"Well, it doesn't matter now," she said. "You'll just have to use mine."

"Yours?"

"You don't think I just burst into private investigators' rooms without a gun, do you?"

"Sometimes?"

Okay, so I was trying to be cute. But the thought of her carrying a gun made me feel somehow submissive. Like a puppy that rolls over on its back when a bigger dog approaches. At least I didn't whimper.

She dug around the dark interior of her camera bag, then said, "Here you go."

She handed me the tiniest automatic pistol I've ever seen. The whole thing fit in my palm. Its trigger guard was outsized to make room for a grown-up's finger, and still was barely large enough to accommodate my big hands. I couldn't help it. I laughed.

"What's this? A cigarette lighter?"

"Very funny. It fires .22-caliber shorts, six shots. It'll do the job if you have to use it. Hell, it gives you something to cover them with, and that's all we need. We'll have the element of surprise on our side."

Gunplay wasn't what I had in mind. Especially not with this little peashooter. The plan I'd silently formulated was to wait for Elvis and Buddy to settle into the house, then go to the nearest phone and call Romero. Then I'd go back to watch the house to make sure they didn't leave before the cops could get there. It seemed like the best plan to me, nice and safe. But something about having the gun in my hand must've made me want to prove my manhood to Felicia Quattlebaum because I said, "Okay."

I instantly regretted it, but there was no backing out. Besides, she was the one who'd found their hideout. She didn't have to bring me along. We could at least give her plan a try. If it looked too risky, I'd just bag it and go call Romero. What could she do without me? I had the gun now.

As I stuck it in my belt, she said, "The safety's on."

"Check."

That was all that was said about it. That was our whole plan.

We chatted a little more about other things, as if we weren't waiting to ambush a dead celebrity. I had just broached the subject of alternate sleeping schedules when I saw the glow of headlights coming from below a rise in the terrain.

"Duck!"

I slid below steering-wheel level and looked over to Felicia Quattlebaum, who had put her camera to her face and was trying to focus in darkness. I grabbed her elbow and yanked her down beside me just as the headlights topped the rise.

I peeked over the dash enough to see the car turn into the driveway of the hideout. It was a dark car, black or navy blue, not the Cadillac. It seemed to be little more than a pair of headlights as it bounced toward the house.

I remember thinking, as we crept through the piñon trees, what if it's the wrong house? What if this goofy editor had the directions wrong? What if we burst in on some innocent family who just happened to be coming home at two o'clock in the morning?

That's what following someone else's plan is all about:

constant doubts about whether they know what they're doing. We're always supremely confident in our own plans. But when following someone else's, there always are misgivings about their competence to lead. And I had every reason to have doubts about Felicia Quattlebaum. She hadn't exactly acted rational since I'd met her, and her own best interests didn't match mine. I took no comfort from the square little pistol that dug into my belly every time I took a step.

When we were close to the house, I whispered for her to stay among the scrubby trees while I checked things out. I hadn't taken three steps before I could hear her behind me again.

Lights had been switched on in part of the house, so I knew where to look. I slunk along a wall in the house's shadow until I came to one of the lit windows, then peeked through the slit between the drapes. I could see a living room with low-backed furniture and dark brown carpet that looked like fur. A glass-topped bar stood in one corner and a bookshelf filled the other. The room was empty.

Felicia Quattlebaum pressed up beside me, trying to see between the curtains, and I moved over so she could take a look. She put her camera to her face and tried to shoot a picture through the narrow gap.

"That's not going to flash, is it?" I whispered urgently.

"Of course not."

The camera clicked and whirred a couple of times. I was torn between trying to look in some more windows and waiting for her to finish. I was just turning away when she grabbed my forearm and pulled me up short.

"It's them," she whispered.

I pushed her out of the way and took a look for myself. Elvis was at the bar, just as he'd been the first time I'd seen him, setting out two glasses for a nightcap. Buddy was nowhere in sight, and I angled my head around so I could check out the corners of the room. Just as I realized where he must be, the drapes parted and light spilled onto my face.

Buddy was to my left, pulling on the cords that opened the full-length drapes. He gaped at me gaping back at him. I reacted like a spotlighted deer and froze for a second. Beside me, I could hear the motor drive on Felicia Quattlebaum's camera whirring, firing off one shot after another.

Buddy reached inside his jacket and pulled out a pistol. Then he yelled something to Elvis, who crouched behind the bar, peeking over the top with wide eyes. Buddy waddled out of the room toward, I presumed, the front door.

"Run!" I yelled, and I took off toward the driveway, figuring it to be the quickest way back to the car. Don't ask me what had happened to Felicia Quattlebaum's plan to capture and interview. One look at Buddy's big revolver had told me we'd lost this arms race, and the angry snarl on his face showed he was willing to use it. Or at least more willing than me. I had the little pistol in my hand, but I figured I needed to be within four feet of a person before I could count on its accuracy. Buddy had no such limitations.

Okay, so maybe I'm rationalizing now. At the time, under those circumstances, it was probably just instinct to run. Unfortunately, Felicia Quattlebaum didn't share those instincts. I was all the way to the driveway, making good time, before I realized she wasn't behind me. I pulled up and looked back and she was still standing at the window, firing away with her camera. Confident, I suppose, that I would protect her. Or maybe just fearless.

"Come on!" I shouted back to her. "Hurry!"

I wheeled my arm at the elbow, as if that would draw her to me faster.

Her camera clicked and switched to automatic rewind

as it hit the last frame. She ran toward me, cameras and equipment bouncing all around her.

"Drop that shit and run!"

"No way," she said, puffing.

I glanced toward the house, then back at her. She'd covered half the distance to me when Buddy burst onto the low-roofed porch, drew down on me with the revolver and shouted, "Thtop!"

I could've made it. If I hadn't halted to yell at Felicia Quattlebaum, I would've made it into the trees and the fat little turd would never have caught up with me. He might've caught her, but I would've still been free to get the cops. Instead, we were sunk.

I said, "Goddamn it."

Felicia Quattlebaum said, "Uh-oh."

Buddy said, "Drop the pithtol."

I was surprised he even noticed the dinky automatic in my hand. I let it fall in the red dust illuminated by the light falling from the open door. Buddy stepped to one side of the door, gestured at us with his revolver, and we marched inside.

The entryway connected via a short hall to the room where we'd spotted Elvis. He was still behind the bar, his knees bent, being careful. He now wore his wide sunglasses like a mask. He straightened up and tucked at his shirt when he saw Buddy had things under control.

"My, my," he said, "if it isn't Bubba Mabry."

I tried to smile.

"Jesus Christ," said Felicia Quattlebaum. "It really is you, isn't it?"

Elvis smiled at her. "No, I'm not Jesus, but I appreciate the comparison."

"You know what I mean." Her cheeks flushed a little.

"Thut up." Buddy prodded me in the back with the pistol.

"I didn't say anything."

"Thut up." Another poke. Why didn't he poke her?

Felicia still had the cameras hanging around her neck and the bag weighing down one shoulder, and Elvis said hospitably, "Why don't I take those for you?"

She grabbed the straps around her neck and her knuckles went white. Her eyes dared him to try it. Buddy cleared his throat to remind her of her situation, and she sighed and handed them over.

Elvis popped open the backs of the cameras, cracked open the film canisters like they were crawdads and began pulling the film out in long curling ribbons.

"So, Bubba," he said without looking up at me, "I thought I could trust you. I never figured you for the type who'd sell me out to the papers."

I tried to look ashamed.

"I didn't really bring her here. She brought me."

Elvis rifled through the camera bag, exposing every roll of film he encountered. He found Felicia Quattlebaum's press badge, studied it, looked up at her and said, "Not a very good likeness, hon."

"Do I look like Miss Photogenic?"

Elvis straightened up and dropped the bag.

"No, you look like someone who could cause me a lot of trouble."

He stepped over to her so his face was close to hers. She squinted up at him, showing no fear.

Buddy touched the barrel of his revolver to my back between my shoulder blades. I stood very still.

Elvis suddenly turned away from Felicia, as if realizing she was studying his face. He returned to the bar and stood with his back to us, mixing drinks.

"Buddy," he said over his shoulder, "why don't you get these folks a couple of those nice comfortable chairs from the dining room?"

I heard Buddy move behind me and the hard circle disappeared from my back, but I didn't turn around.

Elvis faced us, leaning against the bar with a drink in

one hand and a pistol of his own in the other. He cocked the left side of his mouth into a smile.

"Yeah, you look like trouble to me," he said to Felicia. "I've been plagued by people like you all my life. Even now, you people still come snooping around. Buddy and I will have to pick up and move again now. It's hard living like this, running all the time."

Buddy came back into the room lugging a couple of high-backed vinyl chairs from a dinette set. They didn't look comfortable at all. He set them back to back in the middle of the room.

"Thit down." He pulled his revolver from its shoulder holster and waved it at us. We sat.

From a jacket pocket, he produced a coil of thin nylon rope. He handed it to Elvis, who set his gun on the bar. Buddy kept us covered. The sight of the rope gave me hope. Why tie us up if they're just going to kill us?

"Why not stop running?" Felicia piped up. "Go public. You could make enough money to hire an army of guys like Buddy."

Elvis' smile disappeared.

"Not like Buddy," he said. "Buddy's special. Buddy's a true friend, aren't you, Buddy?"

Buddy nodded and drew his rubbery lips into a smile.

I finally found my voice. "Is murder a sign of true friendship?"

Buddy glared at me and threatened with the gun. Elvis said, "What's that supposed to mean?"

"Is that why he killed Tankersley?"

Elvis stepped over to face me. His feet were wide apart so that his face was level with mine. He raised an index finger and pointed it between my eyes, nearly touching my nose.

"We haven't killed anyone," he said. "I wouldn't stand for it."

Felicia said, "Well, somebody killed a great reporter, and I want to know who did it!"

"Thut up."

Elvis looked up at Buddy and cocked a brow.

"Now, Buddy, that's not polite."

"Thorry."

"The cops know all about you," I said.

"Is that so?" Elvis tilted his head to one side. "Well, that's too bad, isn't it? Because by the time they figure out where you are, we'll be long gone. They'll find Buddy's precious Cadillac parked out on a dirt road on the other side of Albuquerque, wiped clean of fingerprints, of course. And that'll be the end of it. We're untraceable."

There seemed to be no reply to that. Elvis shrugged and said, "Now. If you folks will hold real still, I'm going to tie you up."

He did a good job of it. He tied our chairs together, then lashed us to them around the chests and thighs.

Buddy produced a nasty-looking pocketknife and Elvis used it to cut the cord. Then he tied my hands together in my lap and lashed them to my knees.

Felicia growled about how they'd never get away with this and the like, but Elvis said nothing else to us. He disappeared from the room, then came back with a roll of adhesive tape. Felicia was sputtering about her rights as he sealed her mouth shut. He looked me in the eye as he taped my mouth, then gave me a wink.

They left after Buddy wiped the place down for fingerprints. On his way out, Elvis hit a switch on the bookshelf stereo. There was a whir and then the King's voice filled the air, out ahead of a twanging guitar on "Heartbreak Hotel."

Even over the music, I heard their car start up and pull away.

The stereo played most of Elvis' big hits before the compact disc finally gave out. Felicia Quattlebaum and I struggled against the ropes, but we couldn't communicate and nothing worked. Finally, I just relaxed and closed my eyes and tried not to think about Elvis and Buddy maybe changing their minds and coming back to finish the job.

It's probably best that our mouths were taped. I would've hated to hear Felicia Quattlebaum bitch for hours about my flaws.

18

The sun had been up a couple of hours and I was in desperate need of a bathroom by the time Steve Romero walked into the room. His gun was drawn, but he held it loosely alongside his thigh, not really expecting to need it. A couple of dark-uniformed state policemen crowded the doorway behind him, holding their pistols pointed toward the ceiling.

Once he was sure Felicia Quattlebaum and I were the only ones in the room, Romero holstered his revolver and ambled over to us. He shouted over his shoulder for the officers to look around outside.

"And don't touch anything," he reminded them.

They both barked "Right!" and hurried away.

Romero bent over me, looking me in the eye. He gave a sort of shrug with his eyebrows, a sorry-about-this expression, and yanked the tape off my face. The sting took my breath away, but it made me forget about my full bladder for a moment.

"You okay?" he asked.

I worked my lips against the sizzle of the tape for a second before I was sure I could speak.

"Well, I'll never grow that mustache now. All my whiskers have been ripped out by the roots."

"Some women pay a lot of money to have that done." He stood erect and glanced beyond me toward Felicia.

"That's Felicia Quattlebaum of the *Star News,*" I said.

"I know. She's been driving us crazy downtown."

"I'm not surprised."

Felicia tried to talk against the tape, but got nowhere and gave up. I couldn't see her behind me, but I'm sure she was giving off heat.

"How about you untie us?" I said to Romero. "I haven't taken a leak in about eight hours."

"You can't wait until we get some pictures of you in this position?"

"Definitely can't wait."

Romero grinned and produced a five-inch jackknife from his pocket and flicked it open. (Am I the only person in America who doesn't carry a knife?) The knife bit cleanly through the ropes and I creaked onto my sleeping feet and hobbled away toward the bathroom. Romero took his time freeing Felicia and, I noticed as I left the room, let her remove her own tape.

When I returned, Romero's ears were red—as if Felicia had been chewing on them—and she had disappeared from the room.

"Guess she found the other bathroom," I said.

"I guess." Romero shook his head, as if it still buzzed with Felicia's rebukes.

"So how'd you find out we were here?" It was the one question that had come to me in the bathroom.

"A guy called me on the phone. Had sort of a speech impediment?"

"That would be Buddy."

"He said you were in need of some help, then gave me the directions."

"And you hurried right over."

"Of course. I've been looking for you. Captain Morgan's been riding my ass to bring you downtown for a meeting. Didn't you get my messages?"

"I've been tied up."

"Funny. You know, Morgan's not going to be happy when he finds out you've been playing detective while avoiding us."

"Tell him I said happiness has to come from within."

"Yeah? Why don't you tell him yourself? We'll go see him when we're finished here."

Felicia Quattlebaum stormed back into the room, her head snapping around like she was looking for the SWAT team.

"I want to speak to your boss," she said to Romero.

"Good! I'm sure he wants to talk to you." His voice dripped false enthusiasm. These two were not hitting it off. "But you'll just have to wait until the crime-lab people get here. In case you've forgotten, there's been a kidnapping here."

It was time that Romero knew all, but I just couldn't bring myself to tell him. Instead, I said, "Well, it wasn't exactly a kidnapping. We sort of walked into it."

"It's at least false imprisonment and we're going to need to document it. We're not in my jurisdiction now, Bubba. These state police are hot to trot. They've probably called the FBI by now."

"Oh shit."

"That's the way I always feel when it comes to the Feebs, too, but I got nothing to say about it right now."

"The guys who tied us up were my clients," I said. "Every minute that passes, they're getting farther away."

"Can't be helped. It's regulations. I could get an APB out on them."

I hadn't even checked the car when I'd approached the

house. It was all I could do to keep from slapping my forehead.

"It wasn't the Cadillac. It was a dark car. I didn't get a good look at it."

"Too bad." Romero's lower lip pooched out as he nodded, thinking it over. "Sounds like you're up Shit Creek."

"Thanks."

"Don't mention it."

"Officer," Felicia suddenly said, knocking Romero down about three ranks, "what if I were to tell you that the man who tied us up was Elvis Presley?"

That gave Romero pause. He looked over her head to me, and I shrugged and made a face like I didn't know what she meant either.

The Elvis Presley?"

"Of course," she spat.

"Of course." He got out his notebook and a pen. "Why don't you tell me all about it?"

I admired her ability to sum it up quickly. No-nonsense reporting. Romero didn't look up from his notebook until she was done. I noticed she carefully skirted Finkelman and the whole episode on the mountaintop, lying instead that she'd simply spotted Buddy on the highway and followed him here.

"Mm-hmm," Romero said when it was clear she'd finished. He looked at her, his eyes hard, and she nodded, standing firm. Then he turned that look on me and said, "Is that the way it happened, Bubba?"

"More or less," I said, suddenly nervous. "I can't say that the man was Elvis Presley, although there is a resemblance now that you mention it. It's the same man I knew as my client, Mr. Aaron."

I know, it was a chickenshit play, but it was more or less the truth and it was as close as I could bring myself to coming right out and saying it.

"See!" Felicia exclaimed. "Aaron! That was Elvis'

middle name. Aron with one 'A.' It's spelled wrong on his tombstone."

Romero looked back and forth between us, measuring the honesty in our faces. Then he said, "Ms. Quattlebaum, I'd expect a talented journalist like yourself to come up with a better story than this. Especially since you had hours to think about it while you were tied up."

Felicia glared at him. "It's the truth."

"She left out one thing," I piped up, and she turned her glare on me. "Mr. Aaron said they were untraceable because they had ditched the Seville somewhere on the other side of the city."

"The APB's still out on that car. We'll see what it turns up."

There was a pause, punctuated only by Felicia's angry huffing, then Romero said, "That's it? That's all you have to tell me?"

"That's pretty much the way it happened," I said. "I know it sounds screwy, but I think this guy maybe really believes he's Elvis Presley."

"It *is* Elvis, dammit!" Felicia screeched.

Romero's eyes went wide.

In a low voice, I said, "I wish you'd stop saying that."

She sort of growled at me and doubled her fists, but Romero wagged a finger at her to show her to keep her distance.

I was still trying to stretch the kinks out of my muscles. As I bowed my back, I jerked my head toward the hall to show Romero I wanted a meeting. Felicia glared at us while we had our whispered conference. I'm sure she thought I was further eroding her credibility.

"Look, Steve, I think this Buddy character is your killer," I said. "I've talked to him and *he* really believes this guy is Elvis. He's devoted to him. I think Tankersley was about to expose them and Buddy greased him to keep it quiet."

"Did he kill Rodent, too?"

"I don't know."

"I got the ballistics tests back last night. Same gun appears to have killed both of them."

"Then my gun's been cleared?" I felt a surge of hope.

"Yeah, unless the D.A. decides the match is close enough to push it. You're still not off the hook. Morgan's after your ass."

Captain Morgan made that abundantly clear himself during a three-hour session at the police station that afternoon. I drove Romero and Felicia there in my car, though I guess we were officially in custody the whole time. We waited around on hard benches, drinking coffee, until Morgan got out of a meeting. Then I waited some more while a gang of Homicide dicks questioned Felicia in Morgan's office. By the time it was my turn, I'd gotten a pretty good grip on myself and felt ready to take them on.

The cops were not amused by the Elvis story. If only Felicia Quattlebaum hadn't felt compelled to tell them about Elvis. It put me in a bad position. I could back her up on everything but the most essential ingredient—Mr. Aaron's true identity. I just couldn't bring myself to take that step.

I warned Morgan at one point that he was going to give himself a heart attack, but he didn't appreciate the advice.

Finally, after we'd gone through the story eight or nine times and Morgan was going hoarse, they turned me loose. I rode the elevator down to the tiny, guarded lobby, my head humming with questions and answers and evasions and omissions.

I was surprised to find Felicia Quattlebaum waiting for me. She was sitting with her camera bag on a bench outside the door, puffing on a cigarette and watching the traffic. Cigarette butts littered the ground around her feet. Having spent more time than I care to remember at the police station, I could just imagine the parade of criminals, bums, misfits and crude cops she'd witnessed in the past few hours. She didn't look relieved to see me, though. She just squinted up at me through her cloud of smoke. My stomach flopped, and I braced myself for the onslaught I expected for not backing her up on the Elvis deal.

"You all right?" she asked. "You look like they've run you through the wringer."

"I feel a little wrung out. What are you doing still hanging around here?"

"Waiting for you. My car's back at your place."

I didn't point out the taxicab parked across the street.

"Come on. I'll give you a lift."

We walked to the parking garage with the shuffling gait of the sleepless, cranked up the old Nova and drove out Central toward the Desert Breeze.

"So," she said after we were clear of Downtown, "what did you tell them about Elvis?"

Here it comes, I thought.

"Just what I said before. That it looks and sounds like him, but I can't be a hundred-percent sure."

She nodded. I felt my shoulders wincing up toward my ears protectively, but still she didn't let me have it.

She didn't speak again until we were passing the string of garish fast-food joints around the university.

"I'm famished. How about you?"

"Yeah, I'm starving. You, uh, want to get something to eat?"

She studied me for a second, just long enough to load her answer with unclear meanings, then said, "Sure."

I regretted the invitation as soon as it was out of my mouth. She was controlling herself pretty well so far, but why test it? Why spend any more time with her than absolutely necessary? I glanced over at her, at the way her mussed hair framed her face and the big glasses slipped down her nose. She was staring out the window, lost in thought, watching the storefronts slip past.

Nob Hill, with its rejuvenated shops and cool neon signs, has some of the tonier restaurants in town. Places with names like Scalo and Cafe Zurich and Chez What. Places that call themselves bistros, as if that would make you forget they're in Albuquerque, New Mexico.

Albuquerque's a casual town, but I judged that we both looked a little scraggly to drop in at the places where the elite meet to eat. Instead, I asked her, "You like Mexican food?"

"Anything."

I circled the block and went back to Baca's, a family-owned restaurant that's occupied half a block along Central since 1949. No cappuccinos or exotic ice creams or abstract art there. Just red flocked wallpaper and steaming platters of food and the most grotesque carved wooden bar in North America, complete with dragons and stained-glass insets.

It was midafternoon, and there were few customers. Waitresses folded napkins and chatted quietly in Spanish, enjoying the calm before the nightly crush of big appetites.

Felicia Quattlebaum followed me to a booth in the dim back room by the bar. Later, I knew, a guitarist would soddenly serenade these tables, but it was safe now.

We both ordered Coronas and stared at the padded red vinyl menus, too worn out to talk. I was still edgy, waiting for the storm to break, but Hurricane Felicia seemed to have settled down. I guess the wait outside the police station had given her time to see my side of things.

An elderly waitress brought the beers and took our orders and went away. Felicia folded her hands on the tabletop, tapped her thumbs together and said, "So . . ."

Here it comes, I thought.

"Is this your favorite place or something?" She glanced around at the garish carpet, the dark furniture and the big paintings of conquistadors and Indians that decorate Baca's, taking it all in.

"I guess so." I didn't want to commit to anything. I had to watch myself with her.

"It's nice."

"Well, I don't know if I'd go that far, but the food's good."

We both were stalling, I suppose. What do you say after you've been through a kidnapping together? Been nice sharing ropes with you? Plus, we were exhausted from excitement and lack of sleep and nothing to eat. My thoughts were as scattered as trees in the desert.

Finally, she said, "So, what do you think will happen now?"

"I don't really know. If the cops find them, then everything will straighten itself out. If not, then I'm still in a lot of trouble."

"Isn't there something we can do?"

"I think we've done plenty. Thanks anyway."

The food arrived, quicker than usual, and I used the pause to change the subject. I had an inkling of a plan, something that had occurred to me during the police questioning, but I wasn't about to share it with her.

"So," I said, "shouldn't you be putting together your story?"

"What story? Without photos, it's just another crazy Elvis sighting. Nobody's going to believe that's who killed Hank."

"So what are you going to do?"

"Well, I'll write around it, I guess. Give them a story on Hank's murder, and hold back the stuff about Elvis until we have proof."

"Good luck."

"Yeah, it seems impossible now that they've gotten away."

"Listen, I'm awful sorry about that. I guess I could've handled it better and we wouldn't have been caught."

She looked me over.

"You did all right," she said. "I shouldn't have stayed at that window so long. Maybe we could've escaped."

"Maybe, but old Buddy's pretty quick for a fat boy. And he had us outgunned."

"I don't know if they told you, but the cops found my gun outside where you'd dropped it. They won't give it back to me."

"I know the feeling."

"This food's good."

Unlike a lot of Easterners, Felicia seemed unfazed by the heat of green chile. I considered that a point in her favor.

In fact, I began to see a lot of good points in her the longer we talked. I mean, she still came across as overly aggressive and high-strung, but she had nice eyes behind those glasses and a quick wit that made me laugh. She took off her bulky sweater and I noticed for the first time that she was built nicely for such a tiny woman. By the time we finished the spicy food (and a couple of cold beers each), I had warmed to her considerably. Which only made it more awkward when we got back to the Desert Breeze.

The sky was awash in thin orange clouds. After I parked the car, Felicia busied herself with gathering her camera bag. Two red spots burned on her cheeks, but I couldn't tell whether it was the beer or fatigue or whether she was feeling the same sort of tingle of anticipation in her belly that I was.

"Do you, uh, want to come in for a minute?" I blurted out. "Maybe have another drink?"

She wouldn't look at me. She unlocked the door to her rental car and hefted the bag inside.

"Better not. I'm already half asleep."

"Okay," I said, sounding a little glum in my own ears. "Well, I'll, uh, see you later then."

"See ya." And she was behind the wheel and gone before I could stumble through what a nice time I'd had.

My answering machine awaited with messages from reporters. I let the tape play undisturbed while I horsed off my sneakers and stretched my toes. Once barefoot, I poured myself a healthy drink and lay back gingerly on the bed, letting the fatigue wash over me.

When the messages were done, I rewound the tape and punched the buttons on the phone for the one call I planned to make. I asked for Lydia.

"Hello, Bubba," she said when she came on the phone. "I saw your name in the paper."

"Oh yeah? I haven't seen it."

"It just says you were questioned in that reporter's murder and that you couldn't be reached for comment. What's going on?"

"It's a long story and I don't know that I've got the energy to tell it to you right now. I was up all night last night and the cops grilled me all afternoon."

"So, did you do it?"

"Of course not." I was too tired to be insulted.

"Then you can tell me the rest some other time. What can I do for you?"

"I need the address of a local guy, Jerry Finkelman. He's a concert promoter. His address isn't listed in the phone book."

"Bubba," she scolded, "that's much too easy. He'll be in the crisscross directory. But, since it's a murder case, I guess I'll do it for you. Hold on."

She was back in less than a minute, but I still managed to nearly drop off to sleep.

"You there?" she said.

"Uh, yeah, let me get a pen." I sat up and sloshed my drink on the bedspread and fumbled around until I was ready to write down the address. "Shoot."

She gave me an address in the North Valley, an area of five-acre "ranches" and two-acre homes. I thanked her, promised to give her the details later and hung up.

19

Every time I dozed off, someone knocked on my door. This time, persistent tapping dragged me back to the land of the living and I struggled up onto my elbows and blinked and yawned.

The tapping wouldn't stop, so I shouted from bed, "Who is it?"

I could barely hear the reply through the door, but I heard the words "Bambi Gamble" and that was enough to get me on my feet.

"Just a minute!" I called while I checked my hair in the mirror. My teeth looked okay, though my mouth tasted furry. No time to do anything about it now. I hurried across the room, stopped long enough for a deep breath of nonchalance, then swung open the door.

Bambi Gamble glistened in the light that splashed from my room. She stood with her hands on her hips and one knee cocked in front of the other, all glamour and pose and smoke and mirrors. I recognized it for what it was, and still my heart went boom and flames kindled in my firebox.

She'd worn a skirt this time, a tight little black thing that barely covered the subject, and a hot pink tank top that looked as if it was made of that rubber material scuba divers wear. A zipper running down the front struggled to contain Bambi's bounties, looking like any minute it might go pop-pop-pop-pop and send me to Heaven.

Bambi tossed her head, setting off delicious tremors, and breathed, "Hi. Mind if I come in?"

I didn't trust myself to say anything. I just shuffled backward to make room for her and she sashayed in, passing close enough that I could inhale her perfume and feel her warmth.

She eased into my armchair and crossed her legs ever so delicately, as if trying to keep the tiny skirt pulled down to a ladylike length, as if she didn't know it rode up far enough to show the lacy tops of her dark stockings and the black garters that held them up. My throat closed up, and I had to cough into my fist.

Bambi let her baby blues glide up and down my rumpled bed, as if measuring it for sturdiness, and said, "Were you asleep?"

"No, no. Well, yeah, I guess I had dozed off for a minute."

Amusement shone in her eyes, but she didn't say anything. Just waited for me.

"Would you like a drink?"

"What have you got?"

"Bourbon."

She waited for more choices, then said "No, thanks" when none came.

You probably like drinks with umbrellas in them, I thought. But I said, "Think I'll have a little pick-me-up."

Pouring the drink gave me something to do with my

hands, a moment to compose myself. I had to be on my guard, but how was that possible when the Fountainhead of All Lust sat across the room, swinging her high-heeled foot and watching me with smoldering eyes?

I remembered Felicia's Phil, the fellow who fell for Bambi's seductive ploy. It cost him everything, his job, his reputation. But I also remembered he'd said it had been worth it.

I gulped half the drink, crossed the room and perched on the corner of my bed, keeping some distance between me and Bambi Gamble. We were like two volatile chemicals, giving off gases that would ignite if they mingled.

"So, how's your investigation going?"

That's all she's here for, I told myself, to pump you for information. Don't fall for it. These tempting poses, this passionate air, is all part of her act. This is a woman who's spent her whole life in front of a mirror, studying her own face to master every come-hither look, every nuance of flirtation. She has it down to an art form, but this is no time to become a patron of the arts.

"Not so good. I was up all night last night, with no result, and I spent the day being grilled by the police."

"What happened?"

"Nothing, really. Nothing I can talk about anyway."

She cocked her head, smiled.

"You can tell me."

"Oh, no. I've got enough problems already."

"Well, just tell me this. Have you figured out who killed Hank the Tank?"

"I've got a pretty good idea, but nobody knows where the guy is, so my ideas don't mean much."

"Tell me." Sultry, breathy.

"Nope."

Now will come the pout, I thought, that little moue that says, "Daddy didn't give me what I want." I was wrong.

"You think it's Elvis, don't you?"

His name made me jump to my feet and sort of whirl around to catch my balance.

"Um, uh, Elvis?"

She inclined her head, made a silk purse of her lips.

"You're not going to pretend you don't know anything about him, are you, Bubba?"

"Uh, well, I guess not. How do *you* know about him?"

"Hank the Tank told me all about it in Phoenix. When I heard he was killed here in Albuquerque, I figured there had to be a connection."

"And is there?"

"You tell me."

I opened my mouth, then clamped it shut, afraid of what might leak out.

"Come on, Bubba."

"The truth is I don't rightly know. I think there's a connection, but I have no real proof."

"Tell me what you do have."

She was hijacking my brain with her sexiness, bushwhacking me. I struggled to hold on to what little willpower I had left.

"If you know about Elvis," I said finally, "the police are going to want to talk to you."

"There's no time for that now, Bubba. I want this story. I'm passionate about it."

Expressions of desire come with a side of sultriness and the lipstick of the day. One look at her and I was ready to place my order for more.

I tore my eyes away, tried to think about cold showers and baseball, anything to distract me from my lust. I poured another drink and sipped it, telling myself all the while to take it easy on the booze, it could make me talk.

"So where is Elvis?" she asked casually. "Do you know?"

"Nope. I mean, if it is Elvis."

"You don't believe it's him?"

"How can it be? He's been dead such a long time. How come nobody's seen him before?"

"Plenty of people have. We report it all the time."

"Well, yeah. If you believe them." In my mind, I could see my mother talking sincerely to reporters while they chewed their lips to keep from laughing. "I mean, I'm sure they sincerely think they saw him, but there could be a lot of explanations."

Bambi sat back in the chair, sighed, let her fingers trail down her neck and into her cleavage. She watched me, looking for a reaction, seeing if she was doing any damage to my resolve.

"I believe it's him," she said. "And I think it's the story of a lifetime. I want it."

My toes tingled from lack of blood flow. All my blood was busy elsewhere. I hitched at my jeans to make them more comfortable without being too obvious. But Bambi was like a hawk, coldly measuring the distance between her fleeing prey and his collapse. She ran a taloned hand through her hair.

"What would it take," she began, and I thought, Oh Lord, here it comes, "to get you to help me?"

She uncrossed her legs and didn't bother to press them together. Her hand brushed the corner of her eye, her lip, her chin, as if showing me all the places where I could begin.

"I, uh, don't know what you mean."

"You know what I mean."

She wet her lips and smiled. I felt like I might swoon, like there was no blood left in my head, either. Like my whole being had become my pulsating pocket rocket, my heat-seeking missile. I needed to sit down, but the only seat available was the bed and she might see that as an invitation.

I downed the rest of my drink, took a deep, shuddering breath, and said, "You can't buy me."

"I'm not talking about money."

"I know."

Her smile widened, like she knew she could get anything she wanted from me. She slid forward in the chair, leaned toward me so I could see down her zippered front.

"You could help me out, Bubba, and I could help you."

I wouldn't need much help now, I thought. One touch from this bombshell and I'd explode.

"Why is this so important to you? Unless you get him to go public, nobody's going to believe Elvis is still alive. They'll think your story is just another hoax."

"That's where you're wrong," she said brightly. "This story is bigger than just another sighting."

"You mean because Hank the Tank got killed?"

"No, because I think Elvis is ready to make a comeback."

That made me forget for a moment about the fire between my legs. It was a thought I'd had before. How Elvis looked healthy, tanned and trim, how his voice seemed unchanged by his long "death." Maybe he was ready to face the public again, maybe he missed the adoration.

She was watching for my reaction to her revelation, but I just said, "What makes you think so?"

"Oh, just some things Hank told me, some things I've heard. Did Elvis tell you why he was in Albuquerque?"

"He said he had some business negotiations here." I winced as the words slipped out, and shut my mouth before more could follow.

"Now, see," she teased, "you answered a question and it didn't hurt a bit, did it?"

She thought she had me, but the taunt cooled me off, made me think of the curse of the Cutwallers and what little bit of reputation I might salvage after all this was over.

"Look, the truth is, I can't help you, no matter how much I might want to. I don't know where Elvis is."

"Really?"

"Yes, really. He disappeared last night and nobody's seen him since."

She suddenly looked put out, like I had been wasting her time.

"But that's the one thing I need to know, Bubba."

"It's the one thing all of us need to know. Unless I find him, the cops are going to try to nail me for Hank's murder."

Impatience crossed her face, then disappeared.

"I've got to tell you, Bubba, I intend to find him first."

"That's fine. I don't care who gets the glory. I just want off the hook with the cops."

My heart sank as she got to her feet.

"I guess I'd better get going before the trail gets too cold."

Now that I'd danced out of her clutches, I desperately wanted her to stay. Without gullibility's guillotine blade hanging over me, maybe I could get to know Bambi Gamble. I was willing to overlook her posing and preening, at least for a little while, as long as she couldn't take advantage of me.

"Sure you don't want a drink?"

"No, thanks, Bubba."

"Well, you don't have to run off. Visit awhile."

"I've got to go. I've got to find Elvis. A lot is riding on it."

I didn't know exactly what she meant, but I didn't care. I just wanted to find the right words to keep her here a little longer. The whole encounter was like suffering through an Angie Dickinson movie, two hours of feline posturing, in exchange for that brief nude scene. I wasn't even going to get that.

Bambi Gamble tossed her hair and cut her eyes at me and made my belly quiver.

"It's too bad we couldn't help each other out," she said. "It would've been fun."

How come every time she glided out my door I felt like the wind had been knocked out of me? I slumped onto the bed with a lonesome moan.

20

Sleeping in your clothes is a bad habit to fall into when you live alone, but I was caught off-guard. After Bambi left, I drank some more, trying to extinguish the lust that burned inside me. I paced around my room, sloshing whiskey on my hand, mumbling about reporters and Elvis and women and temptation and disappointment. I finally wore myself out. I set my drink on the night stand, stretched out on the bed and the next thing I knew it was morning.

I took a hot shower to wash away my hangover, pulled on fresh jeans and a black T-shirt and set out to find Jerry Finkelman.

Rio Grande Boulevard is one of those semirural, winding roads that people seek out for Sunday drives. Horses and goats graze here and there and the road is lined by vineyards and gnarly old cottonwoods. Tucked in among all these vestiges of irrigation are rambling houses—adobes, ranch-styles, Swiss chalets and Spanish haciendas—populated by people too rich for me to have ever met. The address Lydia had given me was for an adobe house on a narrow blacktop road that split off from Rio Grande in one of the boulevard's curves. A couple of roan horses romped in a pasture beside the house, and the red Porsche was parked out front.

I parked blocking his car in (an old private-eye trick), rang his bell and studied my murky reflection in the stained glass of the front door while I waited. I looked tired and wan and not exactly respectable, especially in such ritzy surroundings, but I'd do.

Finkelman answered his own door and looked surprised to see me. All he could manage was "Yes?"

"Hello, Mr. Finkelman. I'd like to talk with you."

"Not interested." He tried to slam the door, but my foot was in the way, and the heavy door nearly bowled him over as it bounced back.

"Maybe you'd be more interested in telling the cops what you were doing at High Finance the other night."

Finkelman flinched, thought it over a second, then stepped out of the way.

His house was decorated like his office, all low-slung furniture and futuristic lamps. A few Navajo rugs were scattered here and there for a Southwestern effect. Photos dotted the wall nearest the door. Each showed a grinning Finkelman with his arm around a different bored rock star.

Finkelman wasn't grinning now. He looked a little glassy-eyed and twitchy, as if my appearance had shot his nerves. I flopped onto a sofa, crossed my ankles and made myself at home. He stood near the door, glaring at me, trying to decide what to do next.

"Come on in," I said, as if I was the host. "Have a seat."

Finkelman sat across from me, collected himself, cleared his throat and said, "What can I do for you?"

"You can tell me where to find Elvis and Buddy."

"Who?"

"Don't play dumb with me, Finkelman. I saw you at the restaurant with Buddy. I know that you know about them. Now, just tell me where they are and I'll go away."

"I don't know. I've been trying to find them myself."

"You can do better than that." I casually leaned forward. "Don't make me get ugly."

Finkelman's face flushed, and I knew I'd pushed the right button. A little guy like him would get angry when threatened—the result of a lifetime of being pushed around.

"Look, shithead, I said I don't know and that's that. Now you'd better get the hell out of here."

So maybe he didn't scare easily, but he didn't have to get nasty about it. The idea of roughing him up suddenly appealed.

"Careful, boy," I said. "I'm tired of people dicking around with me. I might just take it out on you."

I heard a door close somewhere in the back of the house. Finkelman's angry expression melted into a grin, and I got an uneasy feeling that things were going wrong.

"You just try it," the little weasel said.

I hesitated about looking over my shoulder, afraid of what I'd see. When I finally worked up to it, I found two beefy old boys who had the thick arms and lank hair of roadies. They both wore faded jeans and T-shirts decorated with screaming skulls and fiery guitars. One smiled to show me how many teeth he was missing. The other cracked knuckles the size of walnuts.

"Mr. Mabry, wasn't it?" Finkelman suddenly could afford to be polite. When I nodded, he said, "I'd like you to meet Snake and Jimmy, my two best employees."

"Which one is which?"

"That doesn't matter much to you now, does it?" Finkelman showed me his pointy teeth.

"I don't know. I've got a thing about snakes."

No one seemed amused. Finkelman continued as if I hadn't said anything.

"You seem to have a problem with sticking your nose in places it doesn't belong. Maybe you need someone to rearrange that nose."

"Tough talk from a little shit like yourself."

I know it sounds like I was just aggravating the situation. But I always figured it like this: If someone is going to kick the crap out of you anyway, what harm can it do to mouth off a little? Maybe it'll distract them.

Finkelman sprang to his feet and stood over me, his breath coming hard. I consider myself something of an expert at pushing people's buttons, but this guy was too easy. He had more buttons than a skyscraper elevator.

"You're a real smartass," he said, "but this time you've fucked with the wrong guy."

"I always did know how to pick 'em."

He jerked his head at the roadies, and big hands closed on my biceps and yanked me up over the back of the couch. I wobbled onto my feet to find Snake and Jimmy standing on either side of me. They twisted my arms around my back, causing me to go up on my toes, and held me there. They smelled like sweat.

Finkelman came around the sofa to get up in my face. I tightened my stomach muscles, expecting the cheap shot. But instead he calmly said something that knocked the wind out of me.

"Kill him. Dump his body in one of the irrigation ditches."

"Whoa, whoa, whoa, wait a minute," I yelled. "There's no sense in getting carried away here. I just wanted some answers."

Finkelman smiled coldly.

"Well, you're about to get one. The last answer you'll ever need. You're going to find out if there's life after death."

I cut my eyes to the two roadies, but neither seemed to

be put off by the idea of murder. Gap-teeth grinned at me; I've encountered corpses that smelled better than his breath.

"This is hardly worth killing somebody over," I said to Finkelman. "It's all a big mistake. Why don't I just walk away and we'll pretend none of this ever happened?"

I have to confess something in me didn't quite believe he was serious. The guy's a shrimpy concert promoter. What does he know about murder? But then, he wasn't the one slated to commit the act. Snake and Jimmy didn't seem to be deep thinkers or people with strong moral codes. From the way they looked at me, I'd be just another heavy load for them to lift.

Finkelman shook his head slowly. "Some people don't know when to leave well enough alone. You shouldn't have come here today."

"I'll agree with you there."

"Get him out of here."

The silent roadies hustled me through the kitchen and out the back door. An old Ford pickup sat in the yard between the pasture fence and a neat stack of new hay bales. They threw me into the cab, then squeezed in on either side of me, Gap-teeth at the wheel.

The truck roared out the driveway and lurched onto the blacktop.

"You boys can't be serious," I said. "You wouldn't kill me just because that little goober told you to, would you?"

The roadies snickered in unison, as if relishing what was to come.

"It's all a gag, right?"

The one with the complete set of teeth let his face go serious and said, "Shut up."

"But I'm just trying to talk some sense into you boys. You don't want the heat of a murder charge. The cops'll be all over you."

"I said shut up."

"I'm just telling you for your own—"

I didn't see the big hand coming. He slapped me across the mouth, hard enough to turn my head half around. Because I was off-guard, a whimpered "Ow!" escaped my lips before I caught myself. If he was that serious about silence, I could accommodate.

The one at the wheel guffawed and yanked at the wheel and said, "How 'bout down here, Jimmy?"

I suppose that was fine by Jimmy because he didn't say anything as we jolted onto a dirt road lined on either side by ancient cottonwoods. I didn't chance looking over at him. One slap in the chops is usually plenty for me.

Snake, whose remaining teeth did resemble fangs, seemed to enjoy making the shock absorbers work. We barreled down the dirt road, the truck rattling as it jounced through washed-out places. The road carried us up onto the low levees that line the irrigation ditches. Brown water flowed swiftly, too wide to jump across. Normally, it would've looked pretty, peaceful, but now it only looked deep.

Snake braked the truck and climbed out. I tried to scramble out behind him, but Jimmy got a handful of my shirt and dragged me out the other side. As soon as my feet hit the ground, I squared up and unloaded a fist into his stomach, trying to catch him unaware. It was like punching a shark. I felt a twinge of pain in my wrist.

Jimmy backhanded me across the face and made me forget about my efforts to fight. I tried to fall, but he had hold of my shirt and he gave me enough of a yank to keep me upright. Then he brought his hand back the other direction, catching me on the other cheek. Blood tasted salty in my mouth.

"Now look here," I managed before the hand came back the other way, snapping my head around.

Snake cackled in the background, but he seemed

remote somehow, as if that last blow had come close to knocking me out. That would be fine, I thought. Some things you'd rather sleep through.

Jimmy must've turned me loose because I reeled around the levee, trying to catch my balance. Snake helped me out by sinking a fist into my belly, which stopped all motion.

He was still laughing, which, as it turned out, covered the sound of an oncoming car just long enough. Jimmy said, "What's that?" Then a Dodge appeared between the trees and slid to a halt behind the truck. I was bent over double, but I looked up to see two plainclothes cops throw open the doors and squat behind them, guns pointing at us.

I tried to hold up my hands, but letting go of my stomach only made me topple over onto my face in the dust.

"Police! Hold it right there," one cop shouted. One of the roadies must've twitched because the other cop said, "Don't even think about it."

The cops patted down Snake and Jimmy and had them in handcuffs before I was able to get to my feet. Which suited me fine. I brushed at my clothes and coughed, still trying to get my breath.

"Looks like we got here just in time."

I looked up to see the square-jawed cop grinning at me.

"They were going to kill me."

"I gathered."

"And throw my body in this ditch!"

The cop still grinned, and I gave up on trying to share my indignation.

"You want to press charges?"

"You bet your ass I do. And I want to go pick up their boss, too. He's the one who ordered it."

"Let's go."

I rode up front with the two detectives, my knees straddling the squawking radio on the center console.

The roadies said nothing in the back, but they didn't look happy.

The other cop, a thin young guy with pale hair, informed me they had been assigned by Romero to follow me. They hadn't been certain that I was in the truck, but figured by the way it had hurried away from the house that something was up.

"Lucky for you we followed, huh?" These cops seemed to be enjoying their rescue a little too much.

"Could've been a little quicker about it."

"Well, we had to wait until both guys hit you, didn't we?" He was smiling. "Otherwise, one of them would've walked on the assault charge. Now we've got them cold."

"Assault, hell, I want these guys charged with attempted murder."

"Let's see what their boss says first."

Finkelman, naturally, was gone. His Porsche was still there, blocked in by my car, but he'd disappeared. I waited out front while the cops searched the grounds. The roadies glowered at me from the back seat.

The cops wanted me to ride downtown with them, but I argued that I didn't want to leave the Chevy unattended at Finkelman's house and they agreed to meet me there. Once in my car, though, I got caught up in examining my split lip in the mirror and decided to go home first and clean it up.

21

My phone was ringing when I arrived, but I didn't pick it up. I stood still, listening for the caller's voice to come through my answering machine. It was Romero.

"Damn! I'm tired of talking to this machine. If you're there, Bubba, shag it on down to headquarters. We want you to explain how Jerry Finkelman is mixed up in this case. We're holding his sidekicks here, but there's no sign of him so far."

He hung up, and I paused long enough to rewind my message tape. Some reporters are more tenacious than others, and there were a few messages from them. There also was an earlier message from Romero, telling me the cops had found Buddy's Cadillac on the West Mesa, wiped clean of fingerprints and stripped by thieves.

But the message that surprised me was from Felicia Quattlebaum. It said she'd been looking for me and gave a number for me to call. Without thinking about it really, I dialed the number.

"Hello?"

"Hi, it's Bubba." Talking, I discovered, made my swollen lip hurt.

"Where have you been? I've been looking all over for you."

"How come?"

"Well, uh, to see where we go from here, what comes next."

"You mean with the case."

"Yeah, sure."

I didn't know how she suddenly had become my partner, but I was willing to play along. The memory of that friendly dinner at Baca's was still fresh.

"Well, I've already been hard at it," I said. "I went to Jerry Finkelman's house this morning."

"Was he there?"

"Oh, yeah. And he wasn't very happy to see me. He had a couple of goons there and he told them to drown me in an irrigation ditch."

"Really?"

"Yes, really. Fortunately for me, the cops were shadowing me and they helped out. But not before one of those boys had tried to change the general shape of my face."

"You're hurt?" I thought I heard a twinge of genuine concern.

"Not too bad. I just came by here to clean up. Then I've got to get out of here. Romero will be sending detectives by to pick me up."

"Come here."

"What?"

"Come to my room. They won't think to look for you here."

It occurred to me that her room was definitely one of the places they'd look for me, but you don't argue with an invitation like that.

"Okay, let me, uh, just dress my wounds and I'll be over in a little while."

She told me her room number at the Hilton and hung up.

I found myself humming as I sorted through my closet for a clean shirt. Then I stripped off the T-shirt and went into the bathroom to wash out my lip. It was split horizontally, along my bottom teeth, rather than through-and-through, and I guess I could be grateful for that. It all depends on how your lip wraps around your teeth on impact. If I'd kept my mouth closed, it probably wouldn't have split at all.

I rinsed it out and the sting made me dance a little jig. Then I washed the rest of my face and rinsed the dust off my forearms. Except for my lower lip, which was swollen and purplish along the cut, I didn't look like I'd just come close to death.

I took San Mateo to the freeway and drove west to where the Hilton rises like a tombstone at the crossroads of I-25 and I-40. After I parked the car, I hustled into the hotel, glancing over my shoulder for any sign of surveillance and finding none.

The Hilton is all made up like a Spanish mission, but I paid little attention to the whitewashed walls or the geometric rugs on my way to the elevators. The idea of meeting a woman, any woman, in a hotel did something to my libido that made me forget this was business. After my encounters with Bambi Gamble, my libido didn't need much help.

I don't know what I was expecting, exactly, but let's just say she wasn't wearing a peignoir when she answered the door. She was in work clothes: khakis and sneakers and a loose-fitting cotton blouse. She stabbed at her mouth with a cigarette and said, "You don't look hurt."

I rolled down my lip so she could examine the cut, as if that was the price of admission. She made a face and said, "Come on in."

Her room faced west, and sliding glass doors offered a view of the black volcanoes on the West Mesa, reaching toward the sky like the stumps of burned, broken fingers. Everything in the room was in different shades of cool blue, from the wintry scenes in the mass-produced paintings to the thick carpet underfoot. The bed was made, but it didn't look crisp, as if Felicia had spread it up herself rather than waiting for the maid. A table with two chairs sat by the windows. The table was buried under a coffeepot, an empty cup, an overflowing ashtray and a stack of newspapers.

"Want some coffee? I could call room service."

"I don't think hot coffee would feel very good on this lip."

"How about lunch? Have you eaten?"

My stomach growled in answer, but I covered it by saying, "Where do you want to go?"

"Sit down. I'll call room service. The *Star News* could at least buy your lunch."

Without consulting me, she dialed and ordered two shrimp cocktails, a chef's salad and a carafe of white wine. It all sounded fine to me. Just the sort of thing I'd order when someone else was paying.

While we waited for the food to be delivered, she quizzed me about Finkelman and the roadies. I tried not to make myself sound too heroic, but she still looked skeptical.

She told me about some of the calls she'd made, to car rental agencies, airlines and hotels, trying to get information on where Elvis might've touched down. She'd come up empty, and was beginning to get a little dejected about her story's future. Naturally, I thought of the one thing that wouldn't cheer her up.

"I talked to Bambi Gamble again."

The mention of the name was enough to make Felicia scowl.

"What did that tramp have to say?"

"She's after your story. She knows about Elvis. She was trying to find out where he'd gone."

"How does she know about Elvis? Did you tell her?" She tensed in her chair, and I sensed the wrong answer would get her springing toward me.

"No, no, I didn't tell her anything. She tried to seduce it out of me, but I'd been warned, thanks to you, and she didn't get anywhere."

"Bambi Gamble tried to seduce you? And you resisted?"

"Is that so hard to believe?"

"No offense, Bubba, but I wouldn't have pegged you as someone with that kind of self-control."

"I've had a lot of experience in these matters."

"Mm-hmm." She smiled at my attempt at haughty professionalism.

"Anyway, she didn't get anything out of me. But I got something out of her."

Felicia cocked an eyebrow at me.

"She told me she thinks Elvis is planning to make a comeback."

"Get outta here."

"No, really. That's what she said. I asked her what made her think that, and she said it was some things she'd heard from Tankersley and other people."

"From Hank? She said Hank told her about him?"

I realized I'd touched a nerve, so I just nodded. Felicia looked around the room for her composure.

"She wouldn't tell me anything else about it," I said. "Except that she was in Phoenix when she talked to Hank, and that she came here after she heard about him getting killed."

Felicia looked thoughtful. "That would mesh with the first time you saw her, but how do we know she wasn't here long before that? In fact, how do we know she's not the one who killed Hank? I told you she'd do anything for a story. She's buzzed weddings in helicopters and pretended to be family to sneak into funerals. And she's slept with God-knows-who-all to get what she wanted. What's a little murder after all that?"

Murder's a bigger step than you think, I thought, but I said, "She didn't seem like the type who'd be capable of it."

Felicia squinted at me.

"How long have you been a private eye? You ought to know by now that people are capable of anything. Even the mildest person, in the heat of passion or greed or jealousy, can sleep with a stranger or stick a blade between someone else's ribs."

"That's not a very optimistic worldview."

"I stopped being optimistic after I became a reporter. You see too many corpses."

"I know exactly what you mean."

Once the food arrived, I soon forgot about the pain in my lip. And Felicia managed to forget about Bambi, though she kept busy speculating about Elvis and Buddy and Finkelman and the connections between them.

She only nibbled at her portion of the shrimp and salad, and I finished it off for her. I don't know if it was the three glasses of wine or the proximity of the rumpled bed, but I felt warm and attractive and replete with possibility. I wasn't all flushed and stiff like I was with Bambi Gamble. I glowed, chatty and charming, despite my fat lip, which made my speech blubbery.

Lust welled up inside me for an instant when she said, "So what happens now?" Then I realized she was still talking about Elvis, and I said, "I don't rightly know. I guess I should go back by my place and check my messages, then go downtown and see Romero. His boys will run me down eventually, and I've been roughed up enough for one day."

"Mind if I tag along?"

And that's how Felicia Quattlebaum ended up in my room when I got the message from Elvis. She stood just inside the door—we were only going to be there for a minute—as the machine played back yet another impatient message from Romero. When Elvis' voice came on, choked with emotion, she moved closer and a notebook appeared in her hand as if by magic.

"Bubba, it's, it's Mr. Aaron," came the strained voice. "Something terrible's happened. Buddy's dead. He, he's been killed. I need your help, or I'm afraid the same thing will happen to me. You've got to come quick."

He gave terse directions to an address in Santa Fe before the machine cut him off. Felicia scribbled furiously, getting it all down.

I hit the rewind button, and Felicia said, "Let's go."

"You think we should call the cops?"

"If we do that, they'll get there before we do. Everybody will get the story. Besides, he said he needed you to come help him, not turn him in."

There was something wrong with that argument, but I was too flustered to sort it out. The wine had fogged my brain, and I was unprepared for such sudden excitement.

"All right, let's do it."

We were halfway to the freeway when it occurred to me that neither of us had a gun. I consulted Felicia, and we whipped into the parking lot of a huge Kmart store and hustled through the fluorescent-lit aisles to the sporting-goods section.

Felicia filled out the paperwork and charged the pistol and shells on her company credit card while I stood anxiously by, checking my watch every minute or so. The salesman rightly seemed suspicious of something in Florida called the "Tropical Import Company," but everything was in order and he had to give us the gun.

On the way out to the Chevy, I asked her about the dummy corporation on the credit cards.

"We do it that way so people can't track us," she said. "You'd be surprised at what some of these celebrity security services can do. We all get new cards with a different company name every few months."

The pistol was identical to the one I usually carried, and I paused long enough to load it before I started the engine. Then I stashed it in the glove compartment and headed for the freeway.

It's only about sixty miles to Santa Fe, the hot resort town of the Southwest, but I rarely go there. Everything costs three prices and it's all just a little too charming for my taste. Give me the grime and crime of Central Avenue. Art galleries and bistros leave me cold. This time, though, Santa Fe promised plenty of excitement, and a thrill of anticipation filled the car as we sped north.

22

Juniper shadows were growing long as we bumped onto the dirt road where Elvis awaited. We'd taken the freeway exit for Old Pecos Trail, the last of three Santa Fe exits, but had turned east onto the old highway rather than west into the city. Hills rolled away in every direction, thick with scrub forest interrupted here and there by mud-colored houses.

Elvis' directions led us to a strange house that sat on a low hill. The central part of the house was a geodesic dome, which poked skyward through the trees. Skylights arranged on the roof looked like two eyes and a smiling mouth. At the top of the dome was an iron weather vane in the shape of a cross.

The dirt road was rutted and I flinched whenever the Nova's bottom dragged. I pictured oil dribbling out from under the car, marking our trail. Felicia Quattlebaum braced herself with one hand on the dash and the other on the door, cursing whenever a particularly fierce bump yanked her against her seat belt.

I let the car slide off the dirt track between two trees before we reached the top of the hill. The ground was dry so I didn't worry about getting stuck. Besides, I was in too big a hurry to think much about what would come later. I just wanted to charge up to that house and rescue the King.

Once again, Felicia followed me through pygmy forest, her cameras jangling. It was easier in daylight and we reached the perimeter of the house's cluttered yard in no time. I held out a hand to halt Felicia and keep us out of sight.

The house had the ramshackle look of many additions, all built by a semiskilled carpenter and plastered with stucco. One wing ambled off to our right and a square addition connected to the dome on the far side. The additions featured round windows and square windows and one bulging, smoked diamond-shaped window like they use to customize vans. Rough beams stuck out at odd angles, suggesting an uneven roof. On the near side of the dome was a small porch. Dozens of crystals hung on strings from the porch's slanted roof, swaying in the wind and splitting the afternoon sunshine into tiny rainbows. Beside the porch stood a concrete giraffe that must've been ten feet tall.

The yard, if you could call it that, was littered with old car wheels and orange crates and lumber scraps. A fat gray cat watched us intently from its perch atop a pink plastic birdbath. A shingle-covered doghouse stood empty at the far side of the clearing, making me nervous for a second, but there was no sign of a dog. The cat looked smug.

Prickly pear cactuses sprouted here and there in the clearing, and deep blue wildflowers danced close to the house. Two cars and an ancient pickup stood empty in the drive.

"I thought Santa Fe was populated by the rich," Felicia whispered beside me.

"And the eccentric," I said.

Past Santa Fe encounters flashed through my mind: a sidewalk painter with a flowing white beard and a perpetual squint, punks with intricate hairdos and ratty black clothes, caftaned New Agers with their self-absorbed mellowspeak. Nothing in Santa Fe—even a house as strange as this—should come as a surprise.

Once we'd checked out the place, there was nothing to do but knock on the door. Elvis was expecting us, and peeking in the windows might just get us shot. I had Felicia stand to one side, and I held my new revolver behind my hip, cocked in case I needed it in a hurry.

I was about ready to give it up when the door finally swung open. It was dark inside, but enough afternoon light slanted through the door to illuminate the hairy little man who stood there. He had shoulder-length salt-and-pepper hair and a beard and he wore an off-white muslin robe that reached to the floor. The light in his eyes made me catch my breath and, for just a moment, I could picture him standing in my mother's kitchen, sharing parables while gulping down peach cobbler.

"Yes?" was all he said.

"Uh, hi, I, uh, I'm Bubba Mabry. I got a phone call asking me to come here."

The man cut his eyes to Felicia and back at me. He looked worried, like he was trying to tell us something without speaking. I realize now he was trying to warn us, but at the time I didn't pick it up because Felicia stepped between us.

"Where's Elvis?" she said. "We know you're hiding him here."

I put a hand on her shoulder and tried to push her out of my line of fire, but she shrugged me off and demanded, "Where is he?"

The man opened his mouth to speak, but the next words came from behind me.

"Drop the gun."

I had a sinking feeling in my chest. I glanced over my left shoulder to find Bambi Gamble pointing a small-caliber automatic at my head. I'd been so caught up with the sight of the man who answered the door that I hadn't heard her slink up behind us.

My pistol thumped on the wooden porch. Bambi smiled. The man at the door clucked his tongue. Felicia sighed and rolled her eyes.

"Hi, Bambi," I said, trying to sound like I wasn't about to wet my pants. "What's this all about?"

She cocked a spandexed hip and waggled the gun in my face.

"Well, it's about money, Bubba. Isn't everything?"

"Aw, Bambi." Like I was disappointed in her.

"Inside."

The dark little man backed away from the door, and we ducked inside. Finkelman stood just to the left of the door, a pistol held at arm's length, where he'd had it pointed at the hippie's head. The gun was a fancy chrome automatic with a long silencer attached. I remembered what Romero said about Hank the Tank likely being killed with a silenced gun, but I didn't have much time to think about it. The interior of the house was too startling.

Shafts of fading sunlight sliced down from the sky-lights. The large, domed room was as cluttered as the yard, filled with stacks of books and vases of peacock feathers and rough iron statues of stick men. On a shelf oozed Lava lamps in red, blue and orange. Crudely carved *santos* peeked out from every niche. Chunks of quartz crystal decorated tabletops, and embroidered pillows covered the ragged furniture. In other words, it was a typical Santa Fe home.

Elvis sat on one of two sofas that faced each other in the center of the room. His wrists were handcuffed and his hands rested on his knees. He looked all shook up.

"Welcome to the party," Bambi sighed, making it

sound like something we'd enjoy. "We've been waiting for you."

We'd stopped just inside the door, so taken by this temple of trinkets, and Bambi nudged me in the back with her gun to get me moving.

Finkelman snatched Felicia's camera bag from her shoulder and let it drop to the floor.

"Hey, be careful with that!"

He motioned her away with the elongated gun barrel. He showed us his pointed teeth as he kept us covered, backing away to stand closer to Elvis. Power glowed in his eyes.

"Everybody have a seat," he said.

The character in the robe hardly seemed to notice Finkelman. "Would anyone like some herb tea?" he offered.

"Shut up and sit down."

The three of us weaved between teetering stacks of magazines to sit on the sofa across from Elvis, with me in the middle. On the rough-hewn coffee table stood a nearly life-size bronze bust of Elvis, a dark mirror-image of the handcuffed King.

I felt like I could barely catch my breath. First, the door is answered by someone whose picture should decorate Bibles, then Bambi and Finkelman get the drop on us, then Elvis Presley is waiting inside, captured.

Finkelman circled behind Elvis and stepped up onto a deck that divided the room. He leaned against a counter that separated the main room from a tiny kitchen. A mirror had been set out on the counter and long tracks of cocaine waited in perfect little rows. He kept an eye on us while he bent over the counter and snorted through a tube.

I'd seen people do cocaine plenty of times, though I don't like it myself. That taste. It's like chewing aspirin. Give me bourbon anytime. Give me one now. But I'd never seen anyone Hoover it up with the relish that Finkelman displayed. Whole lines vanished up his pointed honker. This was a man whose nose was built for cocaine.

Bambi Gamble batted her eyes at him from across the room.

"Jerry loves to do cocaine when he's excited," she said. "It prolongs the rush."

She slithered up behind Elvis and rested a hand on his shoulder, caressing his polyester, testing his heat. The small pistol dangled carelessly in her other hand. She was so in control, so relaxed, the way I'd known she'd be in bed. I guessed that was out now. We seemed to have turned up on opposite sides of this little fandango.

I didn't like the way things were shaping up. And, as usual when I'm in a bad situation, I found myself talking.

"How do you two know each other?" I ventured.

"Jerry and me? Oh, we've known each other for years. We went to college together."

Finkelman straightened up and smiled, his face flushed.

"When I found out from Hank the Tank that Mr. Presley here was alive, I was all ready to write it for the paper. But then I thought, why should they sell a million copies and make all that money, and give me my same old paycheck?"

She waved the pistol around coquettishly while she talked, like it was a fan, a parasol. Despite my trembling fear, I found myself looking at her breasts.

"So I thought, how can *I* make the money? And I instantly thought of Jerry. I knew he'd know what to do."

"Yeah," Finkelman shouted from the counter. "And it's going to work, too, despite you butting in."

Bambi tossed her hair at the interruption, and smiled down at me. I got a chill. Finkelman, soaring with a head full of coke, was dangerous, unpredictable. But Bambi

Gamble was scarier. So at ease, so voluptuous, still tempting while she waved that gun around. It was like Eve keeping you covered with a snake.

Bambi reached out so her fingertips brushed Elvis' hair. He shrugged her away, then looked over at me. His expression softened and he sighed heavily.

"I'm sorry about all this, Bubba," he said. "I shouldn't have gotten you in any deeper. But after Buddy was killed, I didn't know where else to turn."

"What happened to Buddy? How did you end up here?"

Elvis shook his head slightly, and cut his eyes toward Finkelman, but the promoter seemed too busy enjoying his coke rush to care whether we talked.

"Jerry here showed up at the house where Buddy and I were hiding." Elvis spoke slowly, waiting to see Finkelman's reaction, then went ahead when it was clear it was okay. "Buddy made me sneak out the back way and get to our car. I heard shots."

Finkelman chuckled suddenly, and Elvis fell silent.

"Go ahead," Finkelman said, "tell them all about it. It won't matter."

"Well, there's not much more to tell, really. I came here, knowing that my friend Jésus would hide me."

He pronounced the name *Hay-zoos,* but I grasped how it would be spelled and my stomach jumped. Jésus smiled serenely beside me, as if he recognized the effect. Guess he was used to it.

"Yeah," Finkelman suddenly said, "but you didn't know that I knew about this place, did you? Once Buddy was out of the way, I knew you'd come here. It was a simple matter for Bambi and me to drive over here and catch you."

Elvis looked at the floor between his knees. Every mention of Buddy seemed to age him a year. Bambi patted his shoulder.

"You see," she said without looking up at us, "Mr. Presley is going to make a comeback. And we're going to orchestrate it."

Elvis shook his head, but said nothing.

"I'm going to break the story of the century, then Jerry's going to put together a concert tour and new records and we're all going to be bathing in money. We're going to be the new Colonel Parkers, managing Elvis' career. Isn't that right, Mr. Presley?"

Elvis hung his head like a hound dog.

"I've told you I can't do that."

"Oh, but you can. See, that's the beauty of it. I'm going to expose you either way. If you cooperate, we'll all make money. If you don't, then your life is ruined and you'll probably end up in prison for faking your own death."

"They can't prove anything."

Finkelman had eased across the room to stand near Bambi and he said, "It's never going to come to that. Because the man is going to do what we say."

"Of course he is," Bambi purred. "We've been through too much now. Jerry's had to kill people. I've chased Mr. Presley all over Arizona and New Mexico. I even slept with that fat, hairy Tankersley to get the information I needed."

Beside me, Felicia gave an involuntary shudder that I somehow found comforting. Jésus sat as impassively as the wooden saints that stared down at us from the walls.

"Everything was going fine until Tankersley showed up in Albuquerque," Bambi said. "He followed me, took pictures of Jerry. He was in the way."

She touched at her lipstick with a pinkie. Her pistol still dangled loosely in the other hand, and Finkelman suddenly snatched it away.

Bambi whirled on him, her teeth bared, but he raised both pistols to eye level and said, "Get back."

She froze, except for her hands, which clenched and

opened alongside her sculptured thighs. She tried to smile, but couldn't sustain it, so that her bright teeth flashed off and on like a strobe.

"What are you doing, Jerry?" Her lips barely moved.

"What does it look like? I'm taking charge."

"We're partners, Jerry."

"Not anymore. You've got a big mouth, Bambi. You're so busy being sexy and clever that you don't use your brain. I never intended to let you be my partner. I just used you to track down Elvis. Now I don't need you."

Bambi composed herself, flounced her hair, lightly bit her lower lip. She looked at him from underneath her lashes, and said, "But Jerry, we've meant so much to each other."

"Yeah, yeah. Shut up and sit."

Rage crossed her face again, but she brought it under control and stiffly circled the sofa to sit at the end opposite Elvis. Felicia pressed her knee against mine to show me she was savoring the moment.

"There," Finkelman said when Bambi was settled. "That's better. I'm holding the guns and everyone is sitting quietly. Now I just have to decide what to do with you."

He swaggered to the counter, stepped behind it and, watching us carefully, set the pistols on either side of the mirror. Then he bent over it with that vacuum-cleaner nose and made more lines disappear. He was just far enough away that he could plug anybody who made a move toward him.

He said "Aaaah!" and sniffed as he straightened up. He picked up the shiny automatic and wiped his nose with the silencer before turning it back toward us. I was afraid he'd reached a decision.

He wandered over toward us, keeping the pistol pointed at me. He'd left Bambi's gun on the counter. I did a quick count and saw he could still shoot all of us without having to reload.

"You'll never get away with this, you know," I said. "The cops know all about you. Snake and Jimmy are in jail. If you try to go public with Elvis, they'll be all over you."

Finkelman honked and grinned and wagged his gun at me.

"Wrong again, stupid," he said. "By the time they catch up to me, we'll have so much money from Elvis' comeback that we can buy off anybody we want. This is New Mexico. The Third World. Enough money, and you can make any problem disappear."

"Not murder."

"Especially murder."

I opened my mouth to say more, but Jésus rested a warm, delicate hand on my arm to silence me. My skin tingled from the contact.

Finkelman waved the gun at Felicia. "The story alone will be worth millions to the tabloids, right?"

Felicia nodded beside me, but that wasn't enough for Finkelman and he shouted, "Right?"

"Right." Her voice sounded thin.

"Then there's posters of the new Elvis and movies and record deals and concerts. We're going to be rolling in it."

Elvis spoke, his voice low and filled with resignation.

"I told you I can't do it. I can't go public."

He kept his eyes on the floor. He looked more worn down and weary than any man I'd ever seen, as if the mere thought of public life was a great weight he must carry. Something about the way he slowly shook his head told me he wasn't merely refusing to cooperate, but that there was something that would keep him from exposing himself to public scrutiny. It occurred to me once again that the man wasn't really Elvis, that he was an impostor who'd capitalized on his resemblance, taking advantage of the devotion of innocents like Buddy.

Of course, I didn't take time to sort through it. I was

too busy trying to figure a way out of this mess. I thought I saw my opportunity coming when Finkelman strutted over toward us, the gun at his side. He stood over Elvis, who didn't look up.

"You can do it, and you will," he said tightly. "You owe it to the public. You're a fucking cultural icon. Your image is everywhere, like you're some kind of god or something. You owe it to America to make a comeback."

Elvis muttered, "I can't."

"Look," Finkelman said, gesturing toward the bust on the cluttered coffee table, "even Jésus thinks you're worth worshipping. Your face is fucking everywhere, on everything. Now, I'm going to show them Elvis' new face."

Suddenly, Jésus rose. Finkelman stepped back and swung the gun barrel around, but the robed man made no move toward him. He held his bony hands out to his sides in supplication.

"You can't do this," he said calmly. "This man has done nothing to you, or to America. If people want to hold him up as an idol, that is their privilege. But he doesn't owe anyone anything. Each of us must simply try to live his own life the best way he can. If his plan for his life doesn't include a comeback, then you have no right to force it on him."

The argument seemed terribly reasonable to be coming from such a strange little man, but Finkelman was unswayed.

"Who pulled your chain? This may be your house, but I'm in charge here. I've got the gun. Now shut up and let me think a minute."

Jésus inclined his head in a silent, resigned nod, as if he knew what was coming next.

Elvis raised his head to look at Finkelman. There were tears in his eyes.

Well, that was enough for me. I couldn't take it anymore. I leaped to my feet and made a grab for

Finkelman's gun. The move was so sudden, so impulsive, that it took Finkelman by surprise and he stumbled backward. I got one hand on the pistol, but he yanked it away. The coffee table caught me sharply across the shinbones, making me gasp. Finkelman swung the gun at my face, and I found myself stretched on the floor between the sofa and the table, my head swimming.

I looked up to see Finkelman standing over me. The gun barrel was only inches from my nose.

Jésus had been knocked to one side during the struggle. He stood at the end of the sofa, beside Finkelman, practically speaking into his ear.

"You can't do this," he said softly. "No amount of money is worth another man's life."

Finkelman turned and gave Jésus a shove in the chest with his free hand.

"I told you to shut up. What do you know about money and what it's worth?"

Finkelman gestured around the room with his gun, forgetting about me for a moment.

"Look at how you live. The way you dress. This may be enough for you, but life has bigger things in store for Jerry Finkelman. And you and this low-rent private eye aren't going to get in the way of that."

He looked back down at me.

"Now get up. I want you on your feet when I put a bullet in you."

I unsteadily clambered to my feet. Finkelman backed away to stay out of reach, more careful now that he knew how reckless I could be.

He pointed the gun at my chest and said, "This is going to give me a great deal of pleasure."

I remember closing my eyes, not wanting to watch the bullet explode from the end of the barrel. The silenced gun went *pfft* and Felicia screamed and I didn't feel a thing. I opened my eyes to see Jésus between me and Finkelman, falling backward with the force of the gunshot. I don't know whether he'd been going for the gun, or simply trying to protect me, but his white robe was splashed with blood just below his heart. I tried to catch him, but I couldn't get a grip on the muslin robe and Jésus crumpled to the floor.

Finkelman's eyes went wide. Even though he certainly intended to kill all of us, he was as stunned as we were that Jésus had made such a sacrifice.

His back was to Elvis, and he had no warning that he was about to join Jésus. Elvis jumped to his feet, grasped the bronze bust of himself in his handcuffed hands and brought it crashing down onto the back of Finkelman's head.

Finkelman didn't make a sound as he slumped to the floor. The impact caved in his skull, and his head looked flat on one side as he stared up dead from the floor. One nostril leaked blood. The bust of Elvis lay beside him, smiling up at the rest of us, as if happy with the job it had done.

As we stood shocked over the two bodies, Bambi Gamble's high heels clattered away toward the front door. Elvis wheeled, saw that she was running. He scooped up the fallen gun and sprinted toward the front door, but we heard a car engine roar to life before he got there and Bambi was gone.

Elvis turned in the doorway to face Felicia and me. He stumbled forward until we could see his hands trembling on the pistol he pointed at us. He'd suddenly developed a tic in his cheek, and all the twitching and shaking made me nervous about his trigger finger.

He ordered Felicia to fetch the key to the handcuffs from Finkelman's jacket pocket. Felicia performed the task delicately, as if she feared Finkelman might suddenly spring back to life. Not surprisingly, she was trembling, too. I felt like the whole world was quaking.

I stepped past Felicia and Finkelman to where Jésus lay with his arms splayed out to either side. Elvis said,

"What are you doing?" I ignored him as I squatted and checked Jésus' neck for a pulse. Nothing. Unlike Finkelman, who looked very surprised to be dead, Jésus' expression was relaxed, almost peaceful. That somehow made me feel worse.

By the time I got to my feet, Elvis had removed the handcuffs. The gun still pointed in my direction.

"Don't you think there's been enough killing?" It was all I could think of to say.

Elvis' face sagged.

"Do I have any choice?"

"You've got us all wrong," I said, thinking now. "We came here to help you. We don't want to expose you, to put you on exhibit like Finkelman was trying to do."

Elvis looked unconvinced.

"You can just walk out that door and we can forget all this ever happened."

Elvis looked over to where Jésus was sprawled on the floor.

"I can't forget it," he said. "I could never forget what I've done. Buddy's dead. He was my best friend. And now Jésus, who never would've hurt anyone. It's all my fault."

Felicia finally found her voice.

"And what about Hank Tankersley?" she said. "His murder is what started all this."

"I know," Elvis said. "I felt bad when Buddy told me he was dead."

"Did Buddy kill him?" she asked.

"Of course not. You heard that woman yourself. She said Finkelman did it. We didn't kill anyone."

I said, "But you and Buddy were seen at the motel."

"Buddy had this idea that he could scare Tankersley into leaving us alone. We had enough problems already with Bambi and Finkelman trying to blackmail me into going public. We'd been playing them along, making them think I was considering it. But Tankersley was dead when we got there, and I knew we had to get out of town. I sent Buddy to tell Finkelman all deals were off. All we needed was a day or two at that place in Tijeras to cover our tracks, then we would've left and none of this would've happened."

He'd let the gun drop to his side while he talked, but I took little comfort in that. Elvis stared down at Finkelman.

"The man was so excited about the money he could make that he lost all perspective. Jésus was right. No amount of money is worth a man's life."

I saw my opportunity.

"The same is true for us, isn't it? You don't want more blood on your hands. Why not just let us go?"

"You'll tell the world about me." He looked at Felicia as he said it.

"No we won't," I said quickly, not giving Felicia a chance to screw things up. "Besides, who would believe us? It's like claiming that you've seen UFOs or Bigfoot. People would think we're crazy. It'll be the same if Bambi writes this up. You can disappear and nobody will be able to prove anything."

Elvis thought it over. He was too far away for me to try to jump him, and I hadn't had much success with that anyway. Our only hope was that he'd come around.

"Maybe you're right," he said finally. "Maybe there's another way."

He waved the gun at us and said, "Why don't you two sit down?"

Felicia sat very close to me on the sofa and I could feel her warm thigh against mine. Her breath was coming up short, but otherwise she seemed okay.

Elvis sidled around the other sofa, keeping his distance, until he reached Felicia's camera bag. He fished her Nikon from inside, stuck the pistol in his belt and began taking our picture. I imagined what we must look like, pale and scared and our clothes askew. I unconsciously tried to smooth my thinning hair. Elvis knew what he was doing. He snapped off several frames at different lens settings to make sure one would come out. Then he rewound the film, removed it from the camera and slipped it in his pocket.

"I don't get it," I said. "Why the photos?"

"Well, I hate to threaten anybody, but it's like this: If you decide later that you want to blackmail me, or you want to go public with my story, then I'll have these photos as insurance. There are lots of loyal fans out there, people like Buddy who'd do anything for me. If you folks screw up, I can turn your photo over to some of them and they could track you down. Something bad could happen."

He pulled the gun out of his belt and I tensed, even though he'd just said he was going to let us go. Then he backed away toward the door, keeping us covered in case I tried something stupid.

"I'm sorry about all this," he said. Then he was gone.

I heard a car start outside and the crackling of gravel as he drove away. I jumped to my feet and hurried to the door, but by the time I flung it open there was no sign of Elvis or his car. Just a spectacular New Mexico sunset that streaked the clouds with blood.

EPILOGUE

I guess it's clear by now that I've had help in writing this. Felicia Quattlebaum has gone behind me, fixing my grammar and inserting words that I wasn't even sure what they meant. She's been staying with me since this whole Elvis business ended, and I guess you could say we've developed a tenuous romantic relationship (her words).

After Elvis disappeared into the sunset that day, Felicia and I took a few minutes to sort out what we should do. Without Elvis, the cops would never understand how we ended up in the same room with a dead Finkelman and a dead Jésus. We finally decided to wipe down everything we might've touched to get rid of the fingerprints, then we slipped out of the house and trudged down the hill to my car.

A pay-phone call to the Santa Fe cops alerted them to the two corpses. Then Felicia and I returned to the relative safety of Albuquerque and Central Avenue.

Since Elvis took Finkelman's gun with him, Romero

211

was never able to get a ballistics test to match up with the slugs they'd recovered from Tank and Rodent. I told him Finkelman killed them both, but I couldn't prove it without revealing that I'd been at the Santa Fe house. The cops never believed the Elvis connection, of course, but they never got enough to pin the murders on me, either, and they finally stopped following me around.

We watched the newspapers for details about the investigation into the deaths of Buddy and Finkelman and Jésus. The Santa Fe paper tried to make a splash of the killings at the domed house, but no one could figure out the link between Finkelman and Jésus, and the hoopla fizzled.

In fact, the cops never even got a positive identification on Jésus. His neighbors knew him only by his first name. He had no identifying papers in his rambling old house and his fingerprints weren't on file anywhere. Those facts still make me nervous, make me think about Nazareth, Mississippi, and a strange hairy man who changed my mother's life. It had been twenty-five years since I'd gotten my one look at my mother's Jesus, and that had been while they'd led him away in handcuffs, his hair down over his face. Was Jésus the same man? I'll never know. He died before I could ask him.

Felicia knows all about the Cutwallers by now, of course. She says it explains a lot about me. I mostly try not to think about it.

I still have nightmares where I see Jésus' serene face and the bloodied robe, a modern-day shroud of Turin. I feel like his death was all my fault, like Finkelman might not have killed him if I hadn't been so stupid. In a way, I guess, Jésus died for my sins.

These days, I'm just trying to get back to some semblance of a normal life. Felicia gave up her job at the *Star News* so we could write this book, and she's been a real slave driver, practically standing over me while I scratched out these words. She says this exposé will make us rich.

I have my doubts about that. Bambi Gamble's story appeared on the front page of the *Celebrity Tattler*—free of any mention of her involvement in the blackmail scheme, of course—and everybody laughed about it in the supermarket lines and forgot it. I fear we'll get the same response to this book.

Sometimes, I think I'd rather forget the whole thing, not risk the ridicule. I'd like to try to recapture the subsistence-level lifestyle I had before, but Central Avenue, all my old haunts, will never seem the same. They've all been touched by stardust.

And now that I've gone ahead with this book, I'll always be watching over my shoulder for Elvis, or for some rabid fan he's sent to silence us. I'll always know he's out there somewhere.

"A standout...Neil may actually be more interesting than Kinsey and as staunch as V.I. — but with a better love of life." —*Kirkus Reviews*

A Neil Hamel Mystery

RAPTOR

JUDITH VAN GIESON

Now Available from Pocket Books
And Look for

NORTH OF THE BORDER

POCKET
B O O K S